SUMMER JOB TWO

CALVIN TO THE RESCUE

THE GREATEST SUMMER JOB IN THE WHOLE WIDE WORLD

Robert L. Hecker

Published by World Audience, Inc.
ISBN 978-1519109835

©2015, Robert L. Hecker

CHAPTER 1

Actually, what happened wasn't all my fault, although after two weeks on the job at Kimberly Tours I'd began to lose the hollow sensation of stupidity when talking to a potential client. I had almost convinced myself that I could sound as though I knew what I was talking about if the tourists would stop asking the wrong questions. If they would only confine their inquiries to the latest findings in cold fusion experiments or what really caused the fall of the Roman Empire, I could load them up with facts, figures and problematics. Even when it came to travel, I was pretty sure I could mesmerize them with exciting mental pictures of exotic places I'd actually seen such as Idaho Falls or even Lake Tahoe, but when they inquired about the merits of a two week vacation on Australia's Great Barrier Reef or a trek inside a Brazilian rain forest, they put a terrible strain on my old Boy Scout creed to be trustworthy and at the same time loyal and helpful.

After two weeks of carrying home an armful of travel brochures, maps and videos of the most requested vacation spots of the world, I was beginning to absorb enough information to actually create a little more sincerity and confidence in my verbal exhortations. With my high IQ it hadn't taken me more than a week to know all about Boulder Dam and Utah's Monument Valley.

But good intentions can only go so far. When the

3

University of Arizona helped me get a summer job with "Kimberly Tours" in Phoenix, I hadn't realized I might be putting my head in the jaws of physical danger. I discovered this when a muscular man returned from a tour I had sold him and his wife. They had desired a safari in Africa, but I had made one little error. After all, could there be that much difference between a safari in South Africa and someplace called South Apopka? The muscular man seemed to think so, especially since he had lost the use of one arm and his wife was now confined to the isolation ward of some hospital.

Fortunately, I'm a fast learner. In less than a month I'd learned that my vast data bank of knowledge regarding astrophysics did not help much when would-be tourists questioned me about airline schedules or global tourist traps.

So, I wasn't sure what Mr. Kimberly was going to tell me when he called me into his office. I was a little relieved when he left his office door wide open.

As it turned out, the open door gave an erroneous message, because his advice was in the form of a rather loud tirade. However, it was not about the previous South Africa fiasco, nor about that morning when I'd let another potential customer get away. Actually, it hadn't been all my fault. The man and his wife wanted to pet penguins in Antarctica. Being kind hearted, I'd done my best to convince them to go to the zoo instead of spending a small fortune on a journey to some icy glacier because when you've seen one penguin you've seen them all.

4

I realized that Kimberly Tours was not in business to save people money, so I assumed that Mr. Kimberly planned to give me a little fatherly advice regarding economics.

But once again I was wrong.

Although I'm a fast learner, it was difficult to decide whether I was being educated or disciplined when near the end of his near tirade---as I was trying to think of a logical excuse to at least close his office door---that Mr. Kimberly sort of girded up his ample girth, took a deep breath as though he was about to make an unpleasant decision, and said, "Well, I suppose, given enough time, you'll learn."

Instead of being relieved that I hadn't been fired, I suffered a sudden miff. Why had he said 'given enough time'? My brain, working with the precision and speed of a Hadran Collider, had always been able to acquire and organize data with blinding speed and accuracy. I'd even sold two or three couples so well that, instead of stumbling out of Kimberly Tours with a dazed look on their faces, they had signed up for tours as far away as Yellowstone Park

Fortunately, my brain was also beginning to learn when it would be prudent to keep my mouth shut, so I seethed quietly while Mr. Kimberly cogitated. Then he cleared his throat before he surprised me by saying, "I was looking at your resume. You indicated you've had travel experience abroad?"

I blinked. I actually blinked with surprise. "Abroad, sir?" This was certainly an abrupt fork in his castigation road. "You mean out of the country?"

5

He sort of raised his eyebrows. "Of course. That's what 'abroad' means."

Uh-oh. Alarm clanged out a word in my mind: stupid, stupid. Not him. Me. I vaguely remembered that when filling out my employment application, I had sort of fudged my credentials by claiming to have been a world traveler. My thought at the time was that since I was trying for a job at a travel agency, I would have a better chance if I did not indicate on my application that my peregrinations from my home in Idaho only went as far as Lake Tahoe last year and one brief trip to Yellowstone Park with my parents, and that when I was ten years old. Stupid! The slight---and need I say 'innocent'---exaggeration about being a world traveler was now coming back to bite me.

I sucked in my breath and steeled myself for Mr. Kimberly's next pronouncement. Since I was the freshman employee in the agency's four-person office staff, I assumed he was going to hit me with those three words people hate to hear: 'You are fired.'

It didn't help my confidence when he got up and closed his office door. "Before we start," he said as he resumed his seat, "this is strictly confidential."

Well, that ruled out a beating. Bruises are difficult to keep confidential.

On the other hand, the word 'confidential' signaled a certain degree of danger. Apparently, I was not going to be fired, at least not right away. But what, I wondered, could be confidential about traveling?

He certainly had procured my undivided attention.

"Confidential?" I croaked. "Yes, sir."

"I know you've only been with the agency a short time, but in this case that might be an asset. In fact, I think you'd be perfect for this...uh... situation."

Situation? The words "Uh-oh," popped into my head. I stopped holding my breath long enough to say, "Yes, sir."

"Europe," he said. "For about three weeks. Would that be a problem?"

Europe? My mind scampered through the implications. I would love to visit Europe. And I certainly didn't have any pressing activities that would suffer if I were gone a few weeks. I was, after all, on summer vacation from the university until the fall semester, which was why I had been able to take the job in the first place.

There was, however, the matter of my band to consider. I had been playing guitar with a few guys who were trying to put together a garage band, but from the way they winced when I had to play solo, I didn't think they would miss me a whole lot. I had, of course, been planning to return to Idaho Falls to spend a few days with my mom and dad before beginning the fall semester at the University, but being in Europe for less than a month shouldn't interfere with that.

On the other hand, there was Connie. We had been pretty close since last summer when I had met her. We'd both had summer jobs at Lake Tahoe, and she had convinced me I should matriculate with her at the University of Nevada instead of returning to Idaho State. Lately, however, our paths had tended to diverge, and even now while I was expanding my world view through a summer job at a travel agency, she had gone off on a foreign education program to Machu Picchu---or was it Manchuria?

So I smiled confidently at Mr. Kimberly and said, "No problem, sir." Then, like a fool, I added, "I'm ready for any mission you have in mind."

Actually, I thought I was on pretty safe ground. Since Kimberly Tours was a travel agency, I assumed his 'confidential' mission would involve some kind of under cover expedition to check out tourist accommodations in exciting places such as Paris or London or Moscow, maybe even one of those river cruises. Although I was now twenty-one, because of my youthful appearance, superior intellect and savoir-faire no one could possibly suspect me of being a spy---a 'secret shopper,' as it were---for a travel agency.

Mr. Kimberly apparently agreed, because his smile was benevolent as he nodded and said, "Good."

However, he kind of hesitated again before he continued. My quick mental reflexes had long ago picked up on the fact that such little hesitations always implied that a person's next words were not going to make me overjoyed or even average joyed, but more likely, not joyed at all. So now Mr. Kimberly's reluctance to name some glamorous destination sent an icy thread of doubt squiggling through my confidence.

It didn't relieve my anxiety much when he cleared his throat before he said, "Against my better judgment..."---he paused and kind of shook his head---

"I have booked a confidential European tour for a small group."

A tour? What would a travel agency spy do on tour with a bunch of people? And he had said, 'confidential.' What could that mean? Had I taken a summer job with some kind of clandestine CIA cabal? My voice was almost a whisper as I intoned, "A tour, sir?"

"The thing that **worries me**," he continued, "is that this situation **could be a real** feather in our cap. But it cropped up out of the blue. The timing couldn't be worse." He ran the fingers of both hands through his thinning hair, and I could almost see my dreams of Europe evaporating. "Liza Barlow," he continued, "is our only available tour director, but she doesn't have much experience."

Tour director? Was he thinking of making me a 'tour director'? I felt a few neurons of anxiety tinkering with the synapses of my brain. I might be a novice in the travel business, but one thing I had learned was that a so-called 'tour director' was the poor soul who was responsible for all of a tour's logistics such as making arrangements for transportation, per diem, lodgings, etc. etc. etc.

If I had to be involved in a tour, I didn't care how inexperienced this Liza Barlow was. She could have the job. As tour director, she would have all the tour responsibilities riding on her shoulders. All I would have to do was...what? What would be my role? bus driver? plane pilot? baggage handler?

My already skeptical neocortex suddenly cried

out: beware!

Mr. Kimberly's body language sent chilling qualms through my own body. He sat upright in his chair, staring at nothing, drumming his fingers on the top of his desk as though trying to make up his mind about a decision he did not want to make! Not good. Not good at all, not when I considered I was to be the subject of the difficult decision.

It did nothing to warm my qualmish blood when Mr. Kimberly finally stopped drumming his fingers on his desk and his eyes swiveled to focus on me. His voice was a harsh whisper when he said. "What I'm about to tell you must not leave this office. Not now, not ever. Is that clear?"

I nodded, unable to speak as horrific scenarios raced through my mind. Europe he'd said. Confidential. I was to be sent on a secret trip to Europe? When I took the summer job at Kimberly tours I hadn't expected to become involved in some kind of cold war in which I might be given a license to kill like James Bond. The thought conjured up images of chases through narrow, ancient streets with me on a motorcycle and a lovely woman sitting behind me, her lovely arms around me, her lovely hair caressing my cheeks, her lovely lips nibbling at my ears while the bullets of bad guys ricocheted around us.

Wait. Bullets? Real bullets? Would I encounter apposing spies, spies who also would have a license to kill? Spies who were good shots?

Suddenly, the thought of being a spy---even a James Bond---did not seem particularly appealing. It didn't help my nerves any when Mr. Kimberly got up and made sure his office door was firmly closed.

"Tour guide," He said as he sat down behind his desk. "They'll need a tour guide."

Tour guide? Me? My agile mind quickly zigzagged through the tasks expected of a tour guide.

I pictured riding in the open top of a bus with a group of elderly passengers and pointing out celebrity's houses hidden behind hedges. I might be able to handle that if the bus rambled around the streets of Idaho Falls where about all I'd have to point out was the old Gayety Movie Theater and the historic bridge over the Snake River, but...

"Europe?" I blurted. "I confess. I've never been to Europe. I don't know anything about Europe, unless, of course, you'd like to know something about the battle of Hastings in ten-sixty-six or the 'potato' war of seventeen-twenty-one. That's not to be confused with the Irish potato..."

"No, no," Mr. Kimberly interrupted. "Not all of Europe. Only Spain."

"Spain?" My mind quickly tore through its minuscule index of Spanish history: The Inquisition? King Phillip and Isabella? "I'm not up on much after fourteen-ninety-two," I confessed. "You know: like Columbus. But--"

With a wave of his hand he dismissed what I was sure would have been an impressive dissertation.

"Cathedrals," he said. "Castles. People love castles, old buildings, fountains, statues, flamenco, bull fights, like that."

"But," I sort of stammered. "I've never been to Spain."

"No problem. We've got tour books that'll give you all the background you'll need."

"But I don't speak Spanish."

"Not a problem. Everybody in Europe speaks English. Besides, the ones on tour are all Americans."

I didn't care if they were all Greek. I might have been able to dredge up a few pointers on Spanish history when Spain was occupied by Visigoths or Moors, but castles? cathedrals? bull fights? No way.

I was suddenly going to be unemployed.

"I don't know," I said, trying to head off what would be an embarrassing disaster in front of a bunch of tourists. "They'll expect..."

He waved away my trepidations. "The girls have never been to Spain. You don't have to be too precise."

"Girls?" James Bond suddenly burst into view again. "What girls?"

"Oh, didn't I tell you? The tour group is four girls."

I gasped. Girls? My audience would be four girls? They would be beautiful, of course. Incredibly sexy. They would all fall in love with me. I suddenly wished I played the violin. There's nothing like the silken, wistful notes of a love song about broken hearts and wasted tears oozing from the strings of a violin to open a maiden's heart. A piano couldn't do it. Well, maybe, but not as well. A guitar? Not unless you could sing a brokenhearted melody while playing it. A wind instrument like a saxophone? Who ever heard of

12

beautiful woman falling for a saxophone player? And drums... forget it.

However... Some dreadful little part of me felt a peculiar thrill. Forget the violin. You can't even play a flute from the top of a bus. Tour guides only had their mellifluous voices to win lovely hearts and minds. Could I pull it off? I knew nothing about being a tour guide, and even less about Europe. But three weeks or more with four gorgeous girls overcame all my trepidations? A lucky angel had finally landed on my shoulder.

I opened my mouth to shout "Oley!" the only word I knew in Spanish, when a dreadful black hole sucked the angel off my shoulder. Wait! Wait! He hadn't said 'ladies.' He'd said 'girls.'

"How..." My voice stuck in my throat. "How old are these girls? Little kids? Babies? I'm not good with babies."

"No, no," he quickly said. "I understand they're your age: twenty-one, twenty-two. One or two might be in college."

I almost whooped with joy. I not only started to breathe again, the air I sucked in was an elixir of bouquets. Tour guide for four voluptuous girls in glamorous, exotic Spain! My mind reeled from the implications: fandangos, exotic surroundings, palm trees, tropical nights on Mediterranean beaches. I could handle that. The girls probably didn't know any more about Spain than I did. And Mr. Kimberly was right about the tour books. I could bone up on Spain. What I didn't know I could fake. I really was lucky. "I

13

except," I chortled.

"Good." He lifted his index finger. "One thing." The finger pointed at me. I froze. His body language radiated icy cryogenics like the Arctic Circle in mid-winter. His voice was almost a whisper when he said, "What I'm about to tell you must not leave this office. Not now; not ever. Is that clear?"

I had no idea why a tour should be so secret, but it was fine with me. Besides, who would I tell? My mother and father in Idaho Falls? They might be shocked about my going to Europe, but supportive.

"Yes, sir," I chortled. "Very clear."

"As I understand it,"---he paused, and I leaned forward, prepared for the best or the worst---"one of these girls is the daughter of a billionaire, one of the richest men in the world."

I breathed again. I'd been right. I could live with that. Boy, could I live with that!

"She wants to tour Spain incognito," he finished.

I'm sure my eyes suddenly bugged out as what he'd said really sank in. Holy Moly. Wow. Three weeks or more with the gorgeous daughter of one of the richest men in the world?! I would turn on the old Dorsey charm, make her fall in love with me. She would go wild, demand that I marry her. I would refuse, of course, until she begged me. Then, because I wouldn't want to break her heart, I would ignominiously surrender. Me. Little old Calvin Dorsey married to one of the richest girls in the world. I really <u>could</u> live with that.

"What's her name?" I could look her up on the

internet.

"Her real name? I don't know."

"You don't... But you said she's one of the four girls. How could you book her?"

"I told you, she's incognito. She's not using her real name. I don't know which one she is. Nobody knows. Even the other three girls won't know."

I thought about that for a couple of seconds. "The daughter of a billionaire. It shouldn't be hard to spot her. There'll be reporters, photographers...."

Mr. Kimberly almost smiled. "Not if nobody knows about the tour. And even if, somehow, they found out, they wouldn't know which one she was. She'd just one of a crowd."

"A crowd? Four isn't a crowd."

He mistook the stunned look on my face for one of admiration, and his smile turned Cheshire. "Sure it is. Four girls. Four young ladies touring Europe, like dozens, maybe hundreds do every year. If they find out she's out of the country, they won't know where she's gone. And if they even get that far, they won't know which one she is."

"But somebody must know what she looks like."

"Nobody who'll tell. She's spent most of her life avoiding publicity. No interviews. No pictures. If the news got out she was finally coming out of seclusion, the paparazzi would go wild. She demands anonymity."

Paparazzi? Oh, yeah. Those crazy photographers. I nodded. "I can imagine. A few pictures would be worth a fortune."

15

"So," he said. "No one---and I repeat, no one---must know she's on a tour. The entire affair has to be top secret."

I almost smiled. My luck really was changing. The poor girl really had a problem. She would either have to stay cooped up in her home the rest of her life, or sneak in little anonymous excursions like this. But her problem was my good luck.

Another good thing: If no one knew about the tour, I would have no competition. "They won't hear it from me." I said as I made the Boy Scout sign. "Scout's honor."

"Good." His smile was a little tight, but it was a smile. "I knew I could count on you."

I quickly forgot all my concerns. For once Lady Luck was on my side. Alone with four gorgeous girls in glamorous, exotic Spain?! One of whom was a billionaire. What difference did it make what she looked like? HER FATHER WAS ONE OF THE RICHEST MEN IN THE WORLD!

Wait! I sat up straighter. If I didn't know her real name, how could I tell which one she was? I wouldn't want to waste my seduction on the wrong one.

On the other hand, finding out shouldn't be too difficult. Could someone who'd been separated from reality all her life conceal her true identity? She'd probably always been surrounded by a bevy of sycophants. She would be haughty, supercilious. Could a billion dollar heiress shed her ingrained hoity-toity hauteur, subjugate her naturally reclusive personality enough to be just one of the proletariat? Perhaps. If I

16

could fake being a tour guide, she could probably fake being one of us peons.

On the other hand, there were only four of them. It wasn't as though I had to pick her out of about a thousand. All I had to do was use my instincts. There had to be little signs, like wearing a million dollar diamond ring, a Rolex watch or carrying a genuine Versace handbag.

"Don't worry, sir," I said. "I'll make sure she..uh...all the girls have a good time." Boy, would I!

"The problem is..." He hesitated, again running his fingers through his hair, a sign I'd come to realize that was not good.

"The problem is," he repeated. "Think about it. Think of the criminals out there. What do you think they might do if they knew the daughter of one of the richest men in the world was away from home, alone, unprotected."

My rainbow dream suddenly lost a few of its colors. One didn't have to be Einstein to work that one out. "Kidnapping."

He leaned forward. Even his nod was a whisper. "Precisely. So, no one, *no one* must even suspect that she's away from home, let alone on a tour."

Danger. Horrible danger. What if I found out? It could cost me my life.

I suddenly had a mental picture of Atlas with the weight of the world balanced on his shoulders, and I frantically sought a way to share the responsibility. "Liza," I blurted. "Liza Barlow. She might spill the beans."

17

He shook his head. At the same time he got up and began pacing his small office. "She doesn't know anything about it. She thinks it's just another tour. Besides, she's going to have enough responsibility handling four girls. If she knew one of them was the daughter of a billionaire, it might interfere with her job. I'm only telling you so you'll...ah...keep your eyes open." He stopped pacing, and when he looked at me his eyes were hard with threat. "If by chance you should find out which one she is, don't start treating her different from the others. It would be a dead giveaway."

I could understand that. I just wished he hadn't used the word 'dead.'

He put his hand on my shoulder, but instead of it feeling like a fatherly blessing, it felt as though I were Jesus and he was Judas Iscariot.

"Nobody must know," he whispered. "Not me, Not you. Not even Liza. I know I can count on you."

For a moment I had a terrifying picture of myself trying to conceal the illicit knowledge like Galileo trying to conceal the fact that the earth moved around the sun. If, somehow, I did discover her real identity, could I possibly harbor such knowledge without giving away some clue? What had he called it: A dead giveaway?

Something about that word 'dead' really shook my confidence.

Then it occurred to me that all I had to do was keep my mouth shut. When I found out,---and, of course, I would---I wouldn't even have to let the girl

18

herself know that I knew. Piece of cake.

"Don't worry, sir," I whispered. "When I find out, I won't tell a soul"

"Except me."

"You, sir?" Uh-oh.

"I've got to know," he said, his voice rising. "Lawsuits. For my own protection, for Kimberly Tours. So, I want you to find out which one she is. As soon as you do, you're to let me know. Nobody else. Only me. A secure telephone. Don't use the internet."

Some of my euphoria was beginning to wane as my brain found black holes in my dream of utopia. Lawsuits? Kidnapping? People with guns? Possibly an attempt on her life? And nothing between the crooks and the golden girl except little old me?

On the other hand, once I passed the information to Mr. Kimberly, my work---my spy work---was done. I could stay away from the girl until the tour was over and she begged me to marry her. What could go wrong?

Mr. Kimberly went to the door, but he didn't open it. "You understand," he said. "The sooner you find out the better."

I understood, alright. The sword of Damocles would be hanging over my head until I did. "Yes, sir," I said. "When I find out, I'll let you know instantly."

"Excellent. Keep in touch with me. That way you can take proper precautions."

Me? Precautions? Against paparazzi? Lawsuits? kidnappers?

He started to open the door, but when he saw

the look on my face he stopped. "Is there a problem?"

It might cost me my job. But better my job than my life. So I said, "Maybe we should take along a bodyguard? Two bodyguards. Maybe three."

His chin came up. "Bodyguards? No, no. Bodyguards would be a dead giveaway."

I sucked in my breath. There was that word again. Dead? Giveaway? Even three weeks with the richest girl in the world would not be much fun if I ended up supine. Frantically, I searched for a logical way to decline the offer. "You're right, sir. Maybe you should get another tour guide, one with more experience."

He smiled and opened the door. "That's just it, Calvin. Who would suspect someone like you to be a tour guide for one of the richest girls in the world? You're the perfect choice."

The perfect choice to end up being tossed in the Mediterranean Sea in a body bag like old Monte Cristo.

On the other hand, Monte Cristo did alright. What if I rescued the golden girl from a fate worse than being rich? I'd be a hero. She would fall madly in love with me. Her father, her whole family would..."I accept," I cried. "I'll do it."

CHAPTER 2

I assumed I'd meet this Liza Barlow and the four girls at the Phoenix air terminal before we set out on our tour, but I discovered I would be meeting them at the airport in Madrid, Spain. They were flying non-stop from Los Angeles while my plane not only made two stops on the way, but at one of them I had to change planes, which meant I had to go through airport security checks twice.

Fortunately, a year ago, when I'd had grandiose ideas of escaping the stultifying clutches of a lifetime in Idaho Falls, I had obtained a passport that was still valid.

I had also read a great deal about the security ordeal one had to endure at an airport when preparing for an international flight. Even so, at Phoenix I was more than a little shell-shocked by having to go through the security electronic scan three times because the first time I had neglected to take off my watch, and the second time I forgot I had a few pennies in my pocket. The third time I not only made it through, but the plastic container with my shoes, belt, keys, cap, jacket, and carry-on bag also passed inspection.

Actually, there was a little glitch that third time, but it wasn't my fault. At least, I didn't think so. I had simply protested the security man's insistence that I remove a tiny penknife from my key ring and surrender it to him. He was not swayed by my tearful story that the two inch penknife was a memento from my dying mother who when she was an army general had died in Karachi while saving the lives of twenty-seven U.S.

marines and President Kargai of Afghanistan.

After he appropriated my penknife, I thought his subsequent full body pat down was a trifle rougher and more intrusive than was necessary.

The point is that I just made it to the airline's departure gate---naturally, the last gate at the end of what seemed like a mile long corridor---in time to board my plane. I was also a little miffed when I discovered that it was frowned upon for tourist class passengers like me to park myself in the first-class section even if they had empty seats. Also, since I had a window seat, it was a little embarrassing when I was summarily escorted to my proper row in the peasant section, and I had to crawl over two other passengers to get to my seat.

The only good part was that with a window seat I had enough light and solitude during the flight to study my travel books, pamphlets and brochures on the wonders of Spain.

Or rather, I tried to study. But since my only other time being an airline passenger had been last year in the brief flight from Idaho Falls to Reno, Nevada, I was awed by the little time it took during the takeoff run for the huge jet, despite its maximum load of passengers and luggage, to accelerate from zero to more than a hundred-miles-and-hour, then hurl itself into the air. Once in the air and I had begun to breathe again, I practically glued my eyes to the window watching the Arizona landscape expand below.

When we were up so high that the landscape looked like nothing more interesting than unbroken desert, I turned to my studies. Absorbing the plethora of data about Spain was a daunting task. A huge number of famous Spanish cities were covered in the manuals, every one with a must see museum or historical site along with one or more castles and at least two ancient cathedrals. Fortunately, my tour couldn't possibly cover them all in just three weeks. By checking our itinerary, I was able to confine my studies to the wonders in the few major cities we would be visiting such as Madrid, Seville and Barcelona.

Each city's museums and historical sites were, of course, unique, but I soon discovered this was not true regarding cathedrals. Their architecture was amazingly similar with impressive golden alters, stained glass windows and soaring vaulted ceilings, although each seemed to have at least one thing that was touted as their *raison d'être* such as amazing tracery in their rose window or a gold-drenched alter.

Castles were something else. While ancient cathedrals stuck pretty much to the same architecture , castles all seemed to be designed by a different madman, favoring things called machicolations, turrets, portcullises, embrasures, keeps, bastions and battlements that were scattered willy-nilly all over the place. If they had Moorish roots there was always a lot of tile work, mosaics, filigree and fountains.

But I figured that if I memorized a few exotic, castle sounding words like parapet or battlement and threw in a familiar term now and then like drawbridge or moat, I could make it sound as though I knew what I was talking about.

Mr. Kimberly had also given me the names of the four girls---or would it be more politically correct to call them young ladies. Anyway, the names were Dawn McKennsey, Heather Gunderson, Valerie Harding and Maria Napelito. I tried to picture what they would look like, but it was pretty much impossible to have four girls with such different names all looking like Miss World winners. And, of course, there was Liza Barlow. I wondered what she would look like. She was probably about fifty years old and twenty pounds overweight, with the face and disposition of a prison guard.

By the time I deplaned at the Madrid-Barajas Airport north-east of Madrid, I had not only memorized the history of the entire Iberian peninsula, I even knew the history of Spain's King Phillip and Queen Isabella. I also learned that a mausoleum a few miles outside of Madrid with a huge cross on its hilltop dome was where Francisco Franco, Spain's former president, was interred. Although we weren't scheduled to visit the site, if I could think of a way to include such erudite information in my dissertations to the four ladies, it would improve my deception as a legitimate tour guide.

I had selected a flight that would get me to the airport a couple of hours before Liza and the four girls were due to arrive, so I had time to learn which gate they would use to deplane. Since I only had a carry-on bag I didn't have to leave the deplane area and go to baggage claim, so I took a seat where I could not only watch for them as they deplaned but also to keep a wary eye out for any suspicious looking characters who might be lurking around.

When about an hour later, their non-stop plane arrived and passengers began walking out of the deplane ramp, it was easy to spot the four girls. They, of course, had been seated in the first-class section, so they didn't have the worn, harried look I expected to see on main cabin passengers after a long flight. Each had masses of gorgeous hair. Well, three of them did. One of the two blondes sported a short, spiky haircut and probably a couple of tattoos somewhere. The other blonde had straight hair that almost reached her waist. One of the other two had lots of hair that was a dusky-red color that left you uncertain as to whether it was natural or came out of a bottle. The fourth had long, lustrous, coal-black hair with bangs over exotic dark eyes.

They were all dressed like fashion models in either tank tops or short dresses over long trousers or tights that were so tight it seemed they would need some kind of shoehorn to get into them. Hanging nonchalantly from a shoulder, each one carried a leather or cloth bag that was big enough to hold a couple of soccer balls and probably cost more money than I made in a month. And their shoes! Two of them sported colorful, high-heeled sandals that I thought were called mid-wedges. One of the others had some kind of short boots with high heels and chain decorations. The other wore high-heeled, open-toed shoes held on by an array of ankle straps. The long-haired blonde and the red-head sported floppy-brimmed hats in colors that matched their shoes. Actually, three of them did not need the high heels; they had legs so long they would have made a giraffe envious. The third one, the brunet, was a little shorter, but equally breathtaking.

The four of them came along the ramp with that one-foot-in-front-of-the-other bouncy stride models used on a runway.

Instinctively, I tried to match each with one of the four names I'd been given. The three tall girls where a toss up, but the only one that seemed to fit a name was the slightly shorter brunet who I figured was Maria Napelito. That sounded more Italian than

Latino. I hoped I was right. If she knew anything about Spain she would soon find out I was a fake.

I also searched for some sign that would indicate which of them could be the daughter of a billionaire, but they all looked so sophisticated with expensive clothes, pouty lips and sexy eyes, I hadn't a clue. But who cared? All in all it looked as though it was going to be an exciting tour, at least for me.

Then I noticed the fifth girl trailing the others, and I began to change my mind about it being a fun tour. She had to be Liza Barlow.

Surprisingly, her figure was almost as breathtaking, but instead of high heels she wore comfortable slippers. Also the legs of her blue jeans were slightly-less-than-skinny but tighter than trousers---kind of baggy really---, and her pale-purple shirt tucked in her jeans looked like a man's shirt with the sleeves rolled up a couple of turns. Her hair, instead of being a long luscious mass of curls, was bunched up in back in a loose knot from which several strands were trying to escape.

But I had been right about one thing: Even though I judged her to be only a little older than the girls, she looked stern enough to have been a prison guard. And judging by the effortless way she carried a large carry-on bag in each hand she had to be strong. Maybe the bags were the reason why her walk, instead of being the mincing stride of a model, reminded me of a gladiator striding toward the arena with a sword in one hand, a shield in the other, and eyes that seemed to be searching for a victim. All in all she gave the impression of someone not to be trifled with.

I stepped forward, saying, "Kimberly Tours."

I figured that if even one of them had any

misgivings about who would be meeting her, my broad smile would calm her fears.

The four girls stopped, but Liza Barlow, came around them so she ended up facing me, saying, "And you are...?"

"Calvin. Calvin Dorsey." I gave her a Boy Scout salute. "Your tour guide."

The four girls smiled and two of them kind of laughed. "Calvin?" one of them said. "For real?"

I held out my hand to Liza, expecting her to drop the bag in her right hand to give me a handshake. But she didn't so much as acknowledge my outstretched hand. Instead, she jerked her head. "Lets get out of this traffic."

Now, that was a good idea. The way we blocked the aisle, deplaning passengers had to practically push past us. As we moved aside, I had my own bag slung over my shoulder, so I said to Liza, "Let me carry those for you."

She kind of sighed and swung the one in her left hand forward. "Take this one. It's killing me."

When I took it I could see why: it weighted about a ton, and I wondered how she could pack an anvil in a carry-on.

After we moved away from the traffic flow, Liza put down her bag, and I did the same with the one I was carrying. Then she smiled and held out her hand.

"Liza Barlow," she said. Her smile changed her entire face. She was actually rather lovely. But her natural features had been obfuscated by her intense concentration, with her dark brows pulled down over dangerous hazel eyes and her jaw sort of clinched in determination. But when she relaxed, her face smoothed out into nice looking planes and her eyes warmed up nicely. It was a face with character, not really sexy, more like...pleasant. I also noticed that her hair instead of being dark brown was actually reddish brown. Also, without the weight of the bags dragging her down, she was able to stand straight so that she was just as tall as the girls. She certainly wasn't overweight. Despite her slender build, she had good shoulders, which explained how she was able to carry both those heavy bags.

She proved I was right about her being strong when she shook my hand. Her grip almost made me wince.

It was going to be a long walk to the baggage claim area, and after looking at the girls' high-heeled shoes, I commandeer a cart with a driver. It was big enough so we could all pile aboard. Not only did the cart save us a long walk, but the driver also knew where to go.

Seated next to Liza I said, "I guess I'd better find us some kind of limo. A taxi won't be big enough."

"Taken care off," she said. "Local tour company. Empire. They'll have an SUV."

I said, "Oh. Great." I really meant it. Since Mr. Kimberly had said that as a tour manager Liza Barlow was relatively inexperienced, I'd been afraid I'd end up being saddled with most of her job. But so far so good. It looked as though she had things under control. If her no-nonsense demeanor was any indication, there would be few if any problems.

We disembarked at the cavernous baggage claim area, and to my relief, Liza tipped the driver.

Looking around the baggage handling area gave me a sense of satisfaction. Here even the first-class passengers had to stand around like the rest of us minions waiting for their luggage to appear on the turnstile. I also noticed that on the outskirts of the crowd several men holding hand-lettered signs bearing the names of passengers or travel companies, waited for their deplaning charges to find them.

As I stood a little apart from my group watching for their luggage to appear, I noticed two men wearing chauffeur caps and black suits with some kind of logo emblems on their breast pockets rudely pushing through waiting passengers toward Liza and the girls. One man was lean with hawk-like features and a closely-cropped beard and mustache. The other was burly enough to be a professional wrestler with the mean eyes and scowling face to match. The skinny guy carried a sign with the name 'Empire Tours' hand-lettered on it, except that the name 'Empire' was misspelled as 'Impire." I assumed the men were Spanish and their English was not exactly fluent, at least their spelling.

When they got close enough, I heard one of the men say to Liza, "Excuse me, lady. You 'Lizabeth Barrow?"

There was no trace of an accent in his words, and he had her name wrong, which gave me a prickle of alarm.

It must have bothered Liza, too, because she kind of stared at the men for a second before she answered, her eyes shifting rapidly as she took in their clothing and faces. Her voice dripped skepticism as she asked, "Empire Tours?"

The guy who had spoken kind of poked out his chest and pointed at the logo on his breast pocket with his thumb. "Yeah," he said. "Check the sign."

Liza leaned forward to get a closer look at the logo. "It says Fed Ex."

The guy sort of grunted with surprise, then turned his beady eyes to his hulking partner and snarled, "I told you: Empire."

The other guy sort of cringed, saying, "They didn't have no Empire."

The skinny guy put his smile back on for Liza, "Sorry about that. We were told to pick up you and four ladies."

"Who told you?" Liza asked.

The guy pulled a piece of paper out of his shirt pocket and studied it. "It don't say. Just a lady named 'Lizabeth Barrow with four ladies."

I was pleasantly pleased that Liza---or more likely, Mr. Kimberly---had arranged for transportation to be waiting for us, but for some reason I could not conceive of Mr. Kimberly dealing with a Spanish company that would employ such obnoxious-looking men.

Apparently, Liza couldn't either because she said, "Let me see that."

She held her hand out for the paper, but the guy put it back in his pocket, saying, "My writing isn't so good."

I put a supportive hand on Liza's shoulder. "What seems to be the problem?" I kept my voice low but hard enough for the two guys to hear.

"No problem," the skinny guy said. "Who the hell are you?"

"Charles Kimberly," I said. "President of Kimberly Tours. Let me see your credentials."

"Credentials?" he said. "We're freelance. Somebody called. Gave me her name. 'Lizabeth

30

Barrow. That's all I know."

He might have said more, but he was interrupted by a short roly-poly guy wearing a black suit and chauffeur's cap and carrying a hand-lettered sign that bore the printed name 'Kimberly.' His jacket did not sport a logo, but his voice did when he said to the two guys, "Hey! Who you stupidos? These peoples son mío!"

The second of the two men growled and reached for the little guy, but the other one grabbed him, jerking him back, at the same time saying to me, "Sorry about that." He gave his partner a shove and the two of them pushed away through the crowd.

Liza turned her head to look at me, her eyes big. "Who were they?" she said.

"Nobody good." I looked at the little guy who was glaring toward the departing goons. "You know them?"

He turned to look at me, frowning. "No, Señor. I not see them before." He held up his sign and I noticed that under the name Kimberly the words 'Empire Tours' were printed with 'Empire' correctly spelled.

Liza said, "And your name is...?"

"Pepe," he said. "Pepe Aragon. Empire tours." He shifted his placard to his left hand so he could snap a salute with his right. "At your servicio, Señora Barlow."

But after what had just happened I was still a little shell shocked so I said, "Do you have credentials?"

"Credentials? Si, Señor." His big smile told me I had said exactly the right thing. He took a flat leather binder from his jacket pocket and with a flourish, flipped it open and held it out to me. On one side behind a transparent window was his Spanish driver's license and on the opposite side an ornate card from Empire Tours.

I passed it to Liza. "Looks like our man."

She glanced at it, then handed it back to Pepe. She looked in the direction the two men had gone. "Maybe we should call the police."

One of the girls said, "No. This is supposed to be a vacation. I don't want to spend my time in some police station."

Liza said, "What do you think,...uh..Pepe?"

Pepe kind of shrugged "They gone."

I agreed with him and the girl. "Point taken," I said. "However,---"

Before I could suggest that everyone be alert for the two men, one of the other girls pointed to the baggage chute that was spitting about a ton of expensive bags onto the turnstile. "Oh," she squealed. "Our bags. Here they come."

With the help of Pepe and a couple of porters we managed to round up all the bags and get them stored inside a big Mercedes SUV parked in front. After everyone was seated, with Liza in the front passenger seat, me squeezed in with the luggage in the back, the girls sampling the vino contents of a built-in bar, and Pepe expertly wheeling the tank-sized SUV along a four-lane avenue, heading for the distant buildings of downtown Madrid, Liza leaned back over the seat to introduced me to the girls.

"Listen up, ladies" After she caught their attention, she said, "Calvin is our tour guide. He'll be showing us all the most beautiful and fascinating sights of Spain. If you have any questions, he would be

32

happy to answer them." I grinned at the ladies so they would not sense my silent prayer that there would be no questions.

Liza indicated the cute girl with the spiky blonde hair. "This is Dawn McKennsey. Dawn is from Arizona."

I shook her slender hand. "Arizona? Phoenix? Me, too."

"Close," she said. "Tucson." I couldn't tell whether her eyes were hazel with amber tints or amber with hazel tints. But they certainly radiated heat. I sincerely hoped that Dawn would turn out to be the mysterious daughter of a billionaire.

Before I could be too badly burned, Liza went on, "And this...." She smiled at the girl with bronze skin, wide shoulders and sun-bleached, straight blonde hair that hung almost to her waist. "...is Heather Gunderson. Heather is from St Louis."

Heather said, "Hi," and squeezed my hand so hard I had trouble hiding the pain. Wow, she was strong. "Good lats," she said. "You work out?"

"Not enough," I felt lucky to get my entire hand back.

"If you need instructions in...uh...anything," she said. "Let me know."

The way she said 'anything' made me start to make an immediate appointment, but Liza sort of growled so I just gave Heather a silly smile like I believed she was just kidding. But I sincerely hoped that she would turn out to be the mysterious daughter of a billionaire.

Liza indicated the girl with red hair. "This is Valerie Harding. Valerie is from Oklahoma City."

When I shook her hand, I cleverly said. "I'll bet

33

that's in Oklahoma."

She smiled and nodded, but she also kind of rolled her eyes as she said, "What was that? A lucky guess?"

I grinned back. But from the condescending tone of her voice I wasn't sure if I wanted her to be the lucky one. With my luck, by trying to be clever I'd just made the most idiotic mistake of my life.

Liza indicated the girl with the shimmering fall of black hair and the features of a Latina who was leaning languidly against the SUV's door. Under heavy dark eyebrows her fathomless dark eyes studied me with a look that I was afraid was making smoke come out of my ears.

"And this is Maria Napelito. Maria is in from Los Angeles."

Maria did not smile, but when she said, "Hi," her voice had the throaty whisper that many actresses use on television when they're trying to seduce some handsome hunk. I smiled and said hello and wondered what it would be like to be lost in those deep, dark eyes. I sincerely hoped that Maria would turn out to be the mysterious daughter of a billionaire.

Liza again made that kind of growl like a lioness protecting her cubs from a predatory hyena, and I slunk away. The warning was hardly necessary. She did not have to tell me that I had better not get familiar with any of the girls. If I even tried, I would surely be fired, if I lived that long. Still, looking at the four lovely faces and provocative figures, made me wonder if it might not be worth it.

But why even think about it? What millionaires would even give a thought to a tour guide? On the other hand, I had three weeks to change their minds.

Also, they might consider me a mere tour guide, but my real task was to learn which one I intended to marry. That meant I would have to develop a really close relationship with each one, didn't it?

I almost licked my lips in anticipation. After our tour was over I could explain to Liza my reason for coming on to the girls. I would just have to keep her from killing me first.

Apparently, during the long flight from the USA the girls had become close friends, and throughout the more than ten mile ride to the hotel, they bubbled away about their trip and what they hoped to see in Spain. I would have joined the discussion except that I was occupied with listening, hoping for some clue in their conversation or demeanor would tell me which was the pampered golden girl.

But while their conversation gave no evidence of their background, it did hint at their personalities. Dawn McKennsey, judging from the way she seemed to control the conversation, had definite leadership qualities. Valerie Harding had a great sense of humor, laughing and effervescencing like an overheated soft drink. Heather Gunderson, seemed to be more conservative, always ready with apropos logic that sounded profound, at least it did to me. Maria Napelito was quieter, listening more than speaking. The word that came to my mind was 'smoldering.'

Liza? Well, she rarely participated in the bantering conversation, and when she did it was usually to answer a question. She seemed preoccupied with her mission. I could understand that. Being responsible for four pubescent females bursting with energy, curiosity, and allure had to be worrisome. I was glad I didn't have her job.

Listening to them, I tried to discern some clue as to which was the heiress. But like most post-adolescent females the girls changed subjects so haphazardly and spoke so rapidly my masculine hearing had trouble keeping up with the conversation. Even so, they evinced no clue as to which one might be a female King Midas.

Thinking about responsibilities brought to mind those two men who had tried to take over my bevy of ladies. What had been their motive? Were they simply after targets-of-opportunity, or had they somehow learned that one of the girls was worth her weight in gold? If so, did they know which one? Maybe I should have allowed them to drag off one of the girls before I stopped them---or tried to stop them.

Now, watching the four girls talking and laughing, I made a silent vow that I would not allow anything bad to happen to any of them, and I would also do my best to make this vacation one they would fondly remember all their lives.

Surreptitiously looking at their lovely faces and awesome bodies, I was already sure it would be three weeks I would remember all my life, which, judging by the look in Liza's hawk-like eyes, might be a little short.

CHAPTER 3

Signs identified the highway we were on as number eleven. During the long drive to the hotel that had been booked well in advance by Kimberly Tours, I quickly came to admire Pepe's driving skill. While the highway was not overly crowded compared to most U.S. freeways, the Madrid drivers drove as though they were all **NASCAR** students. But their **self-obsessed** method of driving did not seem to bother Pepe, probably because most of their four-wheeled projectiles were about a tenth the size of our big SUV. While the majority of the vehicles zooming around us like mosquitoes were small compared to most American owned cars, the ones that fascinated me most were so tiny they looked as though they had been squashed between a couple of 18-wheelers, but happily buzzed along in their version of automotive insouciance.

One of them in particular caught my eye. I think it was because it wouldn't go away. The other cars, even the little mini-cars either buzzed past us or got lost in traffic we left behind. But this one little two-passenger bug never did pass us. Occasionally, it disappeared in traffic, then I would catch a glimpse of it way in the back as though trying to hide in the pack.

Approaching the city, the traffic got thicker and I completely lost track of it. So did my mind, probably because, as we moved into the city, with its long, sweeping avenues and twisty, narrow-streeted old sections, the girls began plying me with questions about Spain in general and Madrid in particular. I thought I fielded the questions pretty well by calling upon my guidebook studies, although I noticed that

Pepe sort of flinched a few times when I was forced to augment my brilliant dissertations with a little imagination. Even Liza shot me a couple of looks that I was sure signified either wonder at my brilliance or doubt about my sanity. Her consternation did not really bother me. I didn't believe any of the girls would ever use my sometimes slightly skewed lessons regarding Spanish history and architecture in some pedantic treatise.

I did notice that Maria did not ask a single question. She appeared to be content to sit quietly with her back to a window, only turning her head occasionally to look out the window, such as when we turned south at a place I assumed was the old Alcala Gate. She picked a good place to become observant. From my guide books I recognized the huge, 300 acre Retiro Park with its lovely gardens and beautiful lake. Clearly visible was a long Hellenistic-looking colonnade bordering the lake. I pointed out the statue of a man on a horse that topped the colonnade. I think I was only slightly misinforming when I identified the man as Julius Caesar and the name of his horse as Euripides, although Pepe did emit a disconcerting groan.

The girl who asked the most questions was Dawn. Considering that she was a university student it was only natural that she would be the most inquisitive. She seemed vitally interested in the route we were taking and where we were going, occasionally making notes in an iPad. Would someone so rich that she could not survive very well without a smart phone be so inquisitive? How would I know?

Actually, I was very impressed by the city of Madrid as I tried to match what I had learned from the guide books with its plethora of lovely Baroque, Renaissance and Gothic fountains, statues and buildings. While the city obviously had many new structures, it was not unusual to see edifices with histories going back hundreds of years, unlike cities in the United States where even historical places often became victims of a wrecking ball. I did my best to give the correct dates when answering questions, but it seemed to me there really wasn't much difference between 1236 and 1648. I mean, when you go back that far, what's a few hundred years more or less?

My apprehension that our hotel might be one of those six hundred year old relics was put to rest when we finally stopped in front of a beautiful modern hotel that proved to have spacious rooms with wrought-iron balconies overlooking a large park and even a swimming pool on the roof.

It had been nearly 9:00 P.M. when we had arrived at the airport, and past 10:00 by the time we finished checking in at the hotel, but the June days were long and outside it was still twilight. The ladies had been traveling first class, and consequently they'd had dinner during the long flight, but we peons in the main cabin had been lucky to get a small bag of peanuts, so I was famished. Also, on the plane with restless passengers constantly moving in and out of their seats turning lights on and off, it had been virtually impossible to sleep. As a result, my eyes felt sticky and I was uncharacteristically tired. Then I remembered there was something like a nine hour time difference between the time here and Nevada plus our flight time. For me, it was about 7:00 o'clock in the morning. I had not only missed dinner, I had also missed breakfast, lunch and about seven hours of sleep.

As soon as I stashed my one bag in my room, I got on the phone and called Liza's room.

When she answered, I told her I'd like to go somewhere for dinner so I'd be out of contact for awhile. I assumed that, despite traveling first class, she and the girls would be tired after their long trip, and by the time they got their tons of clothes out of their bags they would be ready for bed. But Liza surprised me. "Give us twenty minutes," she said. She didn't sound a bit tired, so apparently I was right: they slept better in first class than we peons did in coach.

"Do you have a restaurant in mind?" she added.

The only restaurant I had in mind was whichever was close. I wasn't too concerned about price. It was all going on Kimberly Tours' tab, within reason, of course. I was sure Mr. Kimberly would stick me with what he considered excessive money if my per diem exceeded his expectations.

But I was supposed to be an expert on Spain, so I lied, "Oh, sure. One of the best in Madrid. I'll meet you in the lobby."

The minute she hung up, I called the hotel concierge. He spoke English, of course, and I ask him about restaurants. At first he touted the hotel's restaurant, but I have a low opinion of hotel food, so I nagged him about good places nearby. He seemed a little miffed, and reeled off a bunch of Spanish names I was sure he knew I could never pronounce let alone locate, so I said thanks and called Pepe who had given me his home number in Madrid.

He gave me the name of a restaurant within walking distance of the hotel, saying he was sure I'd enjoy it, especially their fish. By this time it was

40

pushing 11:00 o'clock and I asked if they'd be open. That gave him a good laugh, and he said, "Señor, this is España. Aqui we no begin la ciena before ten."

I remembered reading about that. In most of Spain they still took siestas, working from about ten in the morning until around two in the afternoon. Then they took lunch, had a nap, went back to work around four and worked until eight or nine in the evening. So, naturally, they ate---and played---late. Well, when in Rome....

By the time I met Liza in the hotel lobby I had actually started to wake up. It was as though my mind had convinced my body that it was all a big mistake and I really had been sleeping for the past ten hours. My body knew it was a lie, of course, and also knew that my mind could not keep up the deception for long. The best thing I could do was gulp down some food and hit the sack. Tomorrow was scheduled to be a full day of sightseeing and I had best be alert.

Liza not only surprised me by looking really chic in boots with heels, long trousers, and a mini-dress. She'd also combed out her hair and it curled around her face as though framing a lovely picture of soft skin and luscious lips.

The only thing that spoiled the picture were her eyes. They still had the suspicious look of a lioness protecting her young.

The four girls with her were dressed like models heading out for a night on the town. I could see that the high-heeled boots or strap-on sandals they were wearing were not designed for much walking, so we took a taxi the couple of blocks to the restaurant.

I was really apprehensive about the restaurant. I had kind of assumed that Pepe would steer me to a low

41

or medium priced place where working men and their families would hang out drinking beer and watching soccer on television sets suspended over the bar.

But no. The place turned out to be one of the Discoteque bars I'd read about in the guide books, which were something like those I'd seen last year in casino night clubs on the Nevada side of Lake Tahoe with booths and tables and a good sized dance floor. There was even a band-stand where eight guys dressed in jeans and white shirts were beating out a fantastic salsa for several dancers cha-cha-chaing around the dance floor.

Most of the patrons looked to be in their twenties or thirties with a few older people trying to keep up. Like in the United States, the women's clothing ranged from sexy mini-skirts to long trousers and expensive looking blouses. The men pretty much looked just like they did in Phoenix: raunchy, even to the blue jeans, tattoos and scruffy whiskers. Everybody had lots of black hair and dark eyes.

With my two-day growth of whiskers, worn jeans and black shirt that I wore with the tail hanging out, I thought I fitted right in. That is until I looked around and discovered there wasn't another blue-eyed, blonde guy in sight, not that I'm all that blonde. But spending time in the blazing Arizona sunshine had given my brown hair a kind of blonde highlight that I thought looked pretty sexy. My scruffy whiskers didn't really cut it. Instead of being the request black they were a kind of washed out brown that made them look as though I'd simply forgotten to shave.

When we walked in I guess my entourage created quite a stir because we got a table right away, and guys appeared out of nowhere asking the girls to dance before they even got to sit down. The girls sashayed onto the dance floor so fast I figured they didn't care a thing about dinner.

All except Liza. She turned down a couple of invitations from guys who ignored the fact that I'd held a chair for her like we were together.

A waiter who was actually dressed like a waiter in a dark suit and with a white towel draped over his arm, took Liza's order for a glass of sherry. I tried to read the menu he had given us, but it was all in Spanish. I figured I couldn't go wrong with seafood and ordered some kind of fish he recommended called rosada---that proved to be delicious---and included fish soup, bread with ham, and tomatoes and vegetables.

Watching the girls salsaing on the dance floor I again tried to pick out which might be the chosen one, but when it came to dancing, there was nothing distinctive about any of them that would make me think she had been brought up wallowing in pamper. I'd assumed that her grandee regimen would have included a few years of ballet or some terpsichorean lessons that would give her away, but, no. Like just about all young, gorgeous women these days, at least, Americans, all four girls danced like they'd spent their entire childhood on a dance floor.

Liza also watched the action, and I thought this might be a good time to broach the subject that had been bugging me.

I opened my mouth to ask her which one of the girls she thought might be the chosen one, until I suddenly remembered that Mr. Kimberly had told me that, for her own good, she was not in on the secret. Even so, I could not conceive of her being in charge of such an unusual tour group without being aware that one of her charges was a little out of the ordinary.

I decided to approach the subject obliquely. "What do you think of the girls?" I said nonchalantly. "They're going to be a handful."

"Why is that?" she asked as though looking after four gorgeous, hormone-laden girls in a place renowned for it's passionate men would be no problem.

"You know," I said. "Sexy girls. Sexy guys."

She turned her head to look at me, and when she spoke her voice was low, but filled with warning. "They better keep their distance."

The way she stared at me before she turned back to stare at the dancers, made me realize that the word 'sex' had better disappear from my vocabulary if I wanted to live.

I should have kept my mouth shut, but the acid of curiosity ate through my better judgment and I said, "Kind of an unusual tour. Did they know each other before?"

That got her attention. "No," she said. "They think they won a free vacation paid for by a charitable grant."

"Free? How is that?"

"Some sort of lottery. I don't know the details."

My guess was that the lottery had been rigged to pick the three lucky girls. I mean, when you're really rich you can do such things, can't you?

"It must have been some lottery," I said. "I bet it was how those two men at the airport found out about the girls."

"Probably just local paparazzi looking for a story. They saw a group of young American girls and thought there might be something there."

"They seemed to know in advance we'd be

there."

She turned to look at me. "I don't know how they found out, but as I understand it, this whole thing, the contest, everything, is supposed to be kept out of the papers. So we don't say anything about it to anyone. Is that clear?"

"Not to worry," I said, "Cross my heart. Hope to die."

Immediately after I'd said it, I wished I could take back the 'hope to die' part. A picture of those two goons at the airport flashed in my mind, and I thought dying might not be too farfetched. Our little charade apparently was not as big a secret as we hoped. And if it wasn't, guess who would get the blame?

At least they had the reason all wrong. If they were just paparazzi who thought their story would be about some gorgeous American girls winning a lottery, I could stop worrying.

With my mind cleared and my energy oozing back, when I'd cleaned my plate and was sipping *café con leche*, I felt as though I could now stand without falling down., so I managed to lure Liza away from a Spanish guy with a goatee who had persuaded her to dance. On the dance floor I launched into my version of a cha-cha-cha. Liza proved to be a really good dancer, and I thought I was doing pretty well, especially when a bunch of the real Madridlenos formed a circle to watch us. Even our brood of girls stopped their hip-swinging stomping to watch.

My self-esteem, however, was not helped when after we'd returned to our table, Liza rushed to the restroom and never did come back to our table. I saw her on the dance floor as I sat alone until almost 2:00 A.M. when she left some guy she had been dancing with and told me it was time to leave.

It did not prove easy to pry the four girls away from their collection of salivating partners. In a mixture of expressive Spanish and raunchy English, the guys insisted that the night was still young and only Americano touristas would leave so early.

But we really were Americano touristas and after Liza paid the check and the taxi arrived, I took my life in my hands to help Liza herd the girls away from the disappointed Lotharios.

During the brief taxi ride back to the hotel the girls couldn't stop laughing and talking about their experiences with the overly friendly guys. It had to be the Spanish night air because they were even friendly to me.

CHAPTER 4

The next morning was 'morning' in name only because the ladies all slept until noon, which fit right in with my own psyche because when Liza called around eleven o'clock I had to practically pry my eyes open.

In the hotel dining room, over what for us was breakfast and where Pepe joined us, Liza, with her usual *la Jefe* persona of *the boss,* was the only one who seemed unaffected by lack of sleep. As tour guide I should have planned our itinerary, but I was saved from displaying my incompetence when, using a map to point out the wonders we were going to spend the day admiring, Liza began giving selections to Pepe. I tried to memorize her selections so I could bone up on them in my guide books between the time we finished breakfast and began our tour.

She must have told the girls we'd be doing quite a bit of walking because when we left the hotel I was glad to see they had discarded their high-heeled shoes for colorful Espadrilles with either flat or low wedge heels.

Liza had planned well so we were able to take the shortest routes between stops, beginning with the magnificent Prado Museum. Since I was sure the Prado would be on our visitor's list, I had done my homework, and as we moved through the incredible displays of art, I was able to keep up a running commentary with only a few imaginative insertions.

"The Prado," I parroted, "is one of the most famous art museums in the world with more than nine thousand works of art, including the famous works of Velazquez, Goya, El Greco, Raphael, Titan, Picasso,

Miro, Bosch and others." Fortunately, none of the girls ask me to identify the 'others' and the paintings all had little plaques under them so I didn't have any trouble identifying each one's artist. By hustling the girls along, I didn't leave much time to answer questions about such Spanish icons as Velazquez, Goya and El Greco. The girls were probably as surprised as I was when Liza told us that EL Greco was really Greek?

After taking in the Royal Guards patrolling the incredibly vast Patio de la America, then the San Francisco el Grande cathedral and the Museo de Historio, by early afternoon I was pretty much on a roll, at least until we hit the more than 600 year-old royal palace. But who could memorize the details of 500 rooms and 23 inner courts.

By room number five I had just about exhausted my banter when, thankfully, the girls got bored with the place and we went to the famous huge Plaza Major in the center of the city. By then it was after 2:00 P.M., lunch time for Madridernos and for us.

The plaza with its surrounding five-storied apartments and homes that have restaurants and shops on the ground floors, was teeming with people, so we were lucky to find an unoccupied large café table under a big umbrella. While we were dining, I thrilled the ladies with a little history of the huge plaza, such as how since 1622 when the plaza was dedicated it has been the center of life in Madrid. In the early days they even had bullfights in the huge plaza. And during the infamous Spanish Inquisition many trials and sentencings had been held in the plaza before those found guilty were hauled away to be burned at the stake. Lately, during the Spanish Civil War in the 1930s, battles fought inside the plaza with guns and cannons

48

almost destroyed the whole place. After the war the plaza was rebuilt, including the surrounding homes and shops.

I thought I was enchanting the girls with my knowledge so I was a little miffed when they simply sat around the table in a silent pout. I should have noticed how their eyes had lit up at the mention of 'shops.'

"What's the matter?" I said. "Did I miss something?"

"I thought we were here to have fun," Valerie said.

"We will," I said. "You'll love the monument to Franco. It's just out of town."

"Who was Franco?" Heather asked.

Dawn said, "Not another museum. I've had it with museums."

"Me too," Valere echoed.

"This is Spain," I countered. "I thought you'd like to know a little of its culture."

Heather kind of flipped her long hair, a gesture of pique that I was sure she used often. "Well," she said, "I don't care about culture."

"Me too," Maria said. "I've already seen all the churches I want to see."

"That's right," Dawn added. "We don't want to see statues and museums."

"So what would you consider fun?" I asked. "Tennis, boating?"

"Shopping," Heather said. "Where are the shops?"

Shopping! I sat staring at them, thinking what a waste of their lives. They could shop in Phoenix. Or more likely, Beverly Hills.

"That's right." Valerie said. "I hear they have

wonderful shoes. Real leather."

It was Liza who said, "Alright, No more cathedrals. But this is not the United States. This is Spain. One of the oldest and most civilized countries of the world, so you're going to see a lot of different things like statues and museums. And you're going to be sampling many different kinds of food."

To my surprise it was Maria who said, "Then can we shop?"

"That's right," Dawn added. "Where are the malls?"

Liza's eyes kind of rolled, but she laughed. "Look around," she said. "This plaza is just like a mall. It's surrounded by shops."

The girls squealed and Valerie said, "Can we go now?"

Liza nodded. "We'll all go. But..." She almost glared at the girls. "The rule is: we must all stick together. Calvin can't go looking for you in every shop."

Calvin? Me? Trying to round up four women while they were shopping would be like trying to round up cats in a dog kennel. "Right," I hastily added. "Stick together." Thinking about going from shop to shop with the ladies made me quickly add, "I'll wait here." The look Liza gave me caused me to add, "You know: hold the table. If somebody gets lost they can come back here."

Liza might have given me a hard time about not going with them, but the girls were already on the move so all she said before she hurried after then was: "Don't go away."

After the ladies hurried off, leaving their sweaters or jackets over the backs of their chairs, I was

50

left sitting alone in the plaza where people practically fought for a table.

I was rather enjoying the respite until I noticed two men enter the plaza through one of its many passageways and stand staring. The plaza was crowded, with virtually every café table occupied and with dozens of people standing or walking all through the plaza. There was even a small band off to one side banging out a salsa beat.

Because of all the activity, my gaze probably would not have been drawn to the two men accept that they seemed so out of place. Instead of being casually dressed like everyone else, they wore dark suits with neckties. One was kind of skinny, the other burly like a wrestler.

In addition they didn't seem to be Spanish. Too coarse-looking. No smiling, laughing or even talking. More like Russians or Hungarians.

But what disturbed me was that they were the same two men who had approached us at the airport.

Well, I shouldn't be surprised to see them here. Everyone who comes to Madrid eventually makes a visit to the Plaza Mayor.

Still, there was something about them that gave me a chill of anxiety. I started to get up to go in search of Liza and the ladies, but then I settled back in my seat. Keeping an eye on the two men would be easier than trying to locate the ladies.

So I ordered a cup of thick, hot chocolate and a churro and tried to keep from dozing off in the warm shade of the big umbrella.

The phone in my pocket beeped. I thought it might be Liza, but it was Pepe. After he'd dropped us off at the Plaza, he'd gone to his home on the outskirts of Madrid and now wondered if we needed him. I considered our schedule for the rest of the day. Even if I could pry the ladies away from shopping, every historic place we planned to visit was within walking or taxi distance, so I saw no reason to ask Pepe to leave home. He would be away long enough when we left Madrid in the morning, so I told him no, and to meet us in the morning as planned to make the trip to Seville.

After we hung up, I wondered if I should have told him about the two men. I could ring him back, but on the other hand, I could be jumping to conclusions. Besides, what could we do about them? Call the police? What would I tell them: that I didn't like the looks of two strangers?

When I looked around I found that the men had disappeared, and that made me even more concerned about the ladies.

My concern was somewhat relieved when a voice behind me said, "There you are."

I knew that voice: Dawn. She plopped down in the chair beside me saying, "I couldn't find you. This is a really big place."

I glanced around. "Where are the others?"

"Shopping. I had to quit."

A tingle of alarm jolted me. "Had to? What happened?"

"Damned new shoes." She swung her feet up on the opposite chair. "I should have known better."

"Oh." I breathed a sigh of relief. She was wearing some kind of spring-looking mini-dress that made it difficult to concentrate on her feet.

"I know how that can be," I sympathized. Well, I didn't really know. I'd never worn shoes with three-inch heels that were decorated with chains and stuff. They looked expensive and made her legs look great, but she was proof that one shouldn't wear new shoes when you were going to do a lot of walking.

She slipped off one shoe and stocking and swung her foot up in my lap. "Would you give it a little rub," she said. "That one really hurts."

I stared at her foot. Give her foot, her naked foot, a rub? It was a lovely foot, about size six or seven I guessed, covered with soft, white skin, the sexy toes tipped with some kind of red, aphrodisiac polish, and all of it attached to a slender ankle that in turn was attached to an exquisite leg also covered with lovely warm throbbing skin. Rubbing that fabulous foot would be like rubbing two sticks together to make fire. Only in this case after about three rubs I would be the one on fire.

I was about to make some lame excuse like my arthritis was acting up when it occurred to me that this might be the foot of a billionaires. I certainly didn't look as though it belonged to someone who stood on her feet all day like a waitress or cashier. This could be my chance to find out if she was 'the one.'

I closed my eyes and, using both hands, started rubbing the sole of the foot since it seemed like the least dangerous place.

"Easy," she said. "Not so hard."

I eased up and pushing her foot down closer to my knees, started what I thought was a sensual massage, thinking it might cause her to drop a few clues.

"Nice foot," I began. "No corns or bunions. What kind of work do you do?"

"Vet," she said. "I usually wear low heels."

"Vet?" She had slid down in the chair and tilted her spiky hair against the chair so that her back was provocatively arched. I tried to keep from ogling her lovely, slender body. She certainly didn't look like a soldier, or was it soldieress? "You mean veteran, like a soldier, carrying those big packs?"

She opened her lovely hazel eyes about half way giving her a lazy sensuous look. "No, no. Not vet veteran. Veterinary. Mostly horses."

"Oh." I began working on her toes, and she sort of sighed. Inwardly, I smiled. It was working.

"Horses," I said. "Kentucky Derby. Race horses?"

"Don't I wish. Farm horses. Farm dogs. Cats. Like that."

"Oh. I thought all farms today used tractors."

"They do, but most cattle ranches still use horses."

"And dogs."

"Right."

"Well, uh, what made you decide to be a vet? You grow up with horses? Like polo ponies?"

She chuckled. "Don't I wish. I grew up on a farm. We had animals. Lots of animals. When my folks retired, they moved to Tucson. I'd been in college, working on being a vet, I finished up my studies in Tucson."

"So you live with your folks."

"Yeah. I'm thinking about getting a place of my own. Got my eye on a few acres down by Tombstone. You know, where Wyatt Earp used to live."

If she were lying she was better at it than I would be, especially that part about Wyatt Earp.

She wiggled her toes. "That feels good. You

54

getting tired? You can do the other one."

I grinned at her. "Not yet." She didn't realize I could rub her feet all day.

She slipped off her other shoe and put her foot up beside the first one, and I began working on it.

Some of the people passing by slowed to stare and some of them smiled. When couples passed by, especially older couples, and the men stared, the woman frowned and hurried them along with an elbow to their ribs.

"You should come to Tucson sometime," she said. "I'll take you to Tombstone. Show you Boot Hill."

I said, "It's a deal." But I knew that if I ever went with her to Boot Hill I would probable end up being buried next to Wyatt Earp or Billy the Kid.

I was beginning to work my way up to her ankles when the other ladies saved me from making a fool of myself by returning. All of them carried packages and were giggling like they had found some real bargains and I remembered again that most women would rather attend a sale than the Paris Louvre.

Even Liza was laughing happily until she saw me with Dawn's naked feet in my lap. I couldn't believe how quickly her mouth went from laughing to resembling that of a snapping turtle, with me being the snapee. Even her eyes had the look of a mama turtle protecting her babies.

"What are you doing?" she said

I quickly pushed Dawn's feet off my lap. "She has a sore foot," I explained. "I was giving it a rub."

"Mine are killing me," Valerie said. "Can you give me a rub?"

55

"Mine, too," Heather said. "I'm next."

I glanced at Maria, kind of hoping that she would also offer her feet, but the look she was giving me contained more suspicion than sexy concupiscence.

Liza brought me back to reality by dumping her packages on the table. "Get your shoes on," she told Dawn. She glanced at her watch "It's after five. If we leave now we can make it to the Reina Sofia Museum."

The four ladies sort of glanced at one another before Dawn groaned and said, "Another museum?"

"Don't they have a Disneyland?" Maria said.

Disneyland? I immediately crossed her off my list as a possible erudite billion heiress. Unless her lack of sophistication was a clever act.

"Let's go back to the hotel," Dawn said. "We can lounge around the pool."

The way she quickly slipped on her shoes made me wonder if her feet really had hurt. Could it be she had just wanted me to rub her feet? Maybe I was more of a Don Juan than I thought.

Liza bit her lip. "We really should take in the Sofia. That's where they have the world's best Picasso exhibit. Including his original 'Guernica.'"

I immediately sized on the opening, carefully watching the girls' expressions. Only someone familiar with expensive works of art would know about Picasso's 'Guernica.' But all the ladies had blank looks on their faces.

"What's a Guernica?" Valerie asked.

Heather giggled. "You've never seen a Guernica?"

Valerie's face reddened, but she laughed. "Not a dead one."

Dawn shook her head. "I've seen a couple of those."

Liza couldn't help but smile. "We'll go back to the hotel," she said. "But if you want to go dancing tonight you'd better take a nap."

"We can nap by the pool," Maria pouted.

"Nap?" Dawn said. "Did you see those men at the hotel? Some are hunks."

"Right," Heather agreed. "I vote for the pool."

Liza turned to me. "I could use a nap. You can stay with the girls?"

Four gorgeous girls in bikinis? I fought hard to hide a happy smile. "By the pool?" I croaked. "Yes, I guess so."

"Alright." Liza picked up her bag. "But don't let them stay there too long. Try to get them in bed."

She saw the silly smile on my face and quickly added, "For a nap."

She said it, but too late. I was already trying to clear my mind of erotic visions, but not trying very hard.

"And no more foot rubs," she added.

She didn't have to tell me. There was far too much danger in those lovely feet.

On the other hand all that shopping must have been tough on their metatarsuses. Maybe it was my humanitarian duty to save them a little pain.

I abandoned the idea. It might save them from pain, but it could put me in my grave.

Walking from the famous Plaza Major, laden with packages, I pulled Liza aside. Keeping my voice low, I asked if while shopping she had seen the two men. She said no, but added, "Why? Did you see them?"

57

"Yes, but only for a minute."

She hesitated before asking, "You think they were following us?"

"No, no," I hastened to assure her. "Everybody comes to Madrid. It was probably just a coincidence they were in the Plaza at the same time as us."

"That's true," she said, but there was a trace of worry in her voice.

"Well, don't worry about it," I said. "We'll be leaving in the morning."

She nodded, and I wondered if she was thinking the same thing I was: who were those guys?

CHAPTER 5

My fantasies about the girls in bikinis did not have a happy ending. Oh, the time spent lounging around the hotel pool with the girls was a dream come true, sort of. I got to ogle the four beauties, but they didn't pay much attention to me. I couldn't really blame them. It seemed that virtually all the handsome hunks within a mile had picked this day to lounge around the hotel pool. The men not only looked rich enough to take the day off, they looked as though they'd spend all their waking hours working out in gyms. Even though I had a pretty good Arizona tan, I had the physic of someone who spend most of his time in class rooms, which was true. At the university I should have gone out for football or basketball, even track. Then maybe I could have become one of those macho jocks.

Actually, I was in pretty good shape. Growing up working on farms and in my dad's lumber yard when I wasn't in school had given me a lot of strength, but for some reason it didn't show. With my slender physic I probably couldn't even be admitted to the university chess club.

My one consolation, when I saw the way the men fluttered around the four girls, was that they were wasting their time. Those beautiful girls belonged to me. Well, sort of. They were a little miffed when I told them it was time to leave, but at least they didn't argue too much, which led me to believe that the girls might be attracted to the hunks, but they also knew who was paying their bills.

The evening went a little better since it was sort

of a clone of the previous night only we didn't stay in one place too long.

Madrid is said to be a city of bars---which turned out to be true, oh so true. But not just bars for drinking. Almost every bar had hors d'oeuvers called *tapas* where, before dinner, one could load up on inexpensive appetizers of cheese and fruit and about a dozen other goodies. Many places also featured a band and a dance floor. But, thankfully, the musicians didn't play any cheek-to-cheek waltzes. Every song was an up-tempo salsa or a wild nuevo flamenco, giving the dancers more of a robotic workout than a dance. As for beverages, the girls were convinced that by sticking to a sweet beer called *Mahou*, augmented by shrimp, crackers and at least twenty kinds of cheese from the *tapa* they could dance all night. It seemed to work for them, but even a ton of cheese, fried shrimp, slices of ham and about a dozen kinds of food I didn't recognize, didn't do much for my body's yearning for sleep beginning at about 11:00 P.M.

Liza was no help. Even she became caught up in the magic of the music, and after a while was flinging her lovely body around the dance floor like one of the professionals on "Dancing With the Stars".

My desire for sleep was not due to the consumption of alcohol. I don't drink at all, even Mahou beer, although I did load up on shrimp, cheese and the other stuff. I had to give up trying to keep up with the macho guys on the dance floor. They never seemed to get tired. I wondered what they did for a living that allowed them to prance around for half the night.

It was almost 1:00 o'clock in the morning before Liza threw in the towel, and we were able to shepherd the inexhaustible goddesses back to the hotel. They looked as though they could have bounced around another couple of hours, but I was barely able to stand up long enough to make it to my bed.

The next morning we all paid the price.

Except Liza,---looking disgustingly radiant as usual---she rousted us out of bed at 8:00 A.M., I was barely able to force myself into a form of locomotion that somehow got me showered, dressed, my bag packed and into Pepe's waiting SUV. I was sure I looked like road kill, but the four girls, oh no!... I couldn't believe it. They looked disgustingly beautiful as though about three hours of sleep was all they needed to regenerate, while I, mister macho, needed my full eight hours just to look human.

I kind of had the last laugh though.

The minute the SUV had left the hotel the girls fell asleep like lovely robots whose batteries had suddenly run down.

Leaving Madrid, heading southeast for Seville, our next destination, Pepe swung off the main highway to drive through the city of Toledo.

I was fascinated by the medieval city. I was sure, it didn't look much different than when it had been the capital of the Visigoth kingdom during the 300 years they ruled Spain until the Moors took over somewhere around 711. The Moors then ruled for almost 300 years before they were finally driven out of Spain in 1085 by some knight named El Cid and his Spanish troops from a province called Catalonia.

I tried to explain this to Liza and the four girls as Pepe, somehow, managed to get us through Toledo's narrow, twisting streets without getting lost, but it would have taken a tour of Beverly Hills shops to get their attention. Even Liza's eyes, that she fought to keep open, kept closing as I droned on. I was a little disappointed; I had studied pretty hard so I could tell them about the old city, and all for nothing. Well, not really for nothing. I was quite intrigued myself by the ancient city with all its old stone buildings, walls and narrow, twisty streets. We sure didn't have anything like it in Idaho.

Even so, it didn't take long for my inner battery to also run low. The only thing that kept me awake was when Liza roused herself enough to ask questions, such as: "Wasn't Toledo multicultural at one time? I mean, Christian, Jews and Moors all living together?"

Digging into my hard-pressed memory, and with a few prompts from Pepe, I told her, "That's right. There were Muslims still living here after the Christians re-conquered the city as well as many Jews before they were exiled from Spain in...uh...1492. So for more than three hundred years you had Moors, Jews and Christians living together. That's why Toledo has old Moorish temples, Christian cathedrals and Jewish synagogues all over the place."

I would have enjoyed spending more time in the fascinating city, but we still had a long way to go before we reached Seville and we had to get moving.

In a way, I was kind of miffed that I hadn't been able to show off my vast knowledge to the girls. I did get one last chance as we were leaving Toledo. The Tagus River almost circles the ancient city, and when we crossed over the narrow river on the beautiful stone-carved San Martin bridge, it gave me an excuse to display my vast but dwindling knowledge of Spanish history. It was a little disappointing that Liza was the only one wide enough awake to even hear me when I began telling the famous story that many people believe about how the conquest of Spain by the Muslim Moors (or at least most of Spain) actually began in Toledo. The story goes that the old Visigoth King Rodrigo, who was Christian, 'took advantage' of the daughter of Count Julian after he saw her bathing in the Tagus river. Count Julian (who was also Christian) wanted to avenge his daughter, but he didn't have a big enough army to take on the Visigoth King. So he enlisted the aid of **Muslims living in Morocco**, North Africa hence the name 'Moors'. The Moors apparently saw a chance to get a foothold in Spain, so they agreed to help the Count against King Rodrigo.

I couldn't remember who won, but I think it was the Count with the Moors' help. The story is that the battle might have started the subsequent Moorish invasion of Spain.

I planned on impressing Liza with my vast, hastily crammed knowledge, but I got sidetracked. What happened is that when we turned onto the main highway leading south toward Seville, I noticed a small, yellow-colored car parked off the road with the hood of its engine compartment up as though it was having engine trouble. The car appeared to be identical to the one I'd seen a few days ago on our trip from the Madrid airport, and I turned my head to look back at it after we had passed. My heart took a jump when I saw a burly man get out of the car and close the car's open hood. I could have sworn he was one of the guys I'd seen in Madrid at the Plaza major. I was not really surprised when the tiny car pulled onto the highway going in our direction.

But even with its three cylinder engine straining mightily, it could not keep up with the big SUV, and I soon lost sight of it in the traffic.

Liza noticed the way I was concentrating on the scene behind us and she said, "What is it? What's going on?"

The four girls were still dozing, and I saw no point in alarming them or Liza, so I turned back as I said, "I thought I saw a Ferrari. But I guess not."

Pepe heard me and said, "Maybe it was a Lamborghini. Once I saw one."

"Maybe," I said. To change the subject, I pointed out the window. "Hey, look at the size of those sunflowers."

Liza gave me a speculative look before she turned her head to look at the fields of sunflowers we were passing. "Beautiful," she said.

"We see many in Andalusia," Pepe interjected.

"Andalusia." Liza said. "We're going to Seville."

"It's a district," I quickly said before Pepe could speak. "The south of Spain. Borders the Mediterranean Costa del Sol."

"Oh," Liza said. "I've heard of that. Isn't that where most of the Moors lived?"

"Right," I said, happy to expound while I could still remember what I had read yesterday in my guide book. "Andalusia is considered the home of real Spain. But I don't see why, because it's where most of the Moors settled after they invaded." I jerked a thumb at a village we were passing where most of the identical white, red-roofed houses were built on the sides of a hill. "See that," I said. "Those villages are called pueblos blancos because almost all the houses are whitewashed, with red tile roofs and lots of fountains. For some reason they're almost always built on hills with a cathedral or a castle of some kind on the top. I

64

guess that's the Moorish influence."

Pepe kind of snorted which I took to mean I might be wrong about the Moors. But it sounded right to me since this whole area had been dominated by the Moors for three hundred years, and the Moors liked white buildings and the sound of running water, hence all the fountains.

Although I was fascinated by the Andalusia landscape and how so much of it reminded me of Arizona's deserts with their vast farms and fields wherever they could get water., the only thing that kept me awake was when he stopped at a small roadside shopping area for lunch and gas. I practically had to carry the sleepy girls from the SUV to the restaurant. They might have perked up if we'd had time to explore the couple of shops that seemed to carry nothing but tourist merchandise, but we had to be on our way.

The thing that really jarred me awake, happened just as we were leaving the restaurant, and I noticed the small yellow car pull into the parking area. My senses leaped to attention when the skinny guy and the burly guy got out and went into the restaurant. Liza was busy herding the girls back to the SUV so she didn't notice them. If Pepe noticed, he didn't mention it.

I was going to call their attention to the yellow car and the two guys, but decided against it. I had no evidence---except for intuition---that their presence had anything to do with us. For all I knew, they were either tourists or business men who just happened to be going the same direction we were. And why yell 'fire' when all I had was a hint of smoke? If there were no fire, I would be considered a fool. If there were, I would deal with it when I saw a flicker of flames. Until then, why spoil the girls' tour with thoughts of....of what?

My only really bad scenario was that, somehow, they had learned that one of the girls was the daughter of an American billionaire and were up to no good. But I had no proof. I would just have to remain on my guard.

Resuming our journey through the area of southern Spain known as Andalusia, I was able to keep my mind from being taken over with bad scenarios by concentrating on the scenery. While the girls napped, I spent a couple of pleasant hours looking at colorful villages, fields of orchards, sunflowers, and crops of some green stuff I couldn't identify. I tried to imagine what the area must have looked like when it was under control of the Moors. I was surprised when, according to my map, we whizzed past the ancient city of Cordoba without stopping.

I had assumed a brief stop at Cordoba would be on our to-do list since one of Spain's biggest tourist attractions was its Mezquita, one of the Moors' largest and most lavish mosques. My guide book has said that when the Christians retook Spain, instead of tearing down the elegant Muslim mosque, they had simply built a Gothic cathedral inside the huge mosque, with room left over.

But looking at the four girls who had only been half-awake the entire trip, I doubted that they would be incensed about missing one more cathedral no matter how unique its splendor.

Liza had been semi-alert throughout most of the trip, gazing out the windows at the passing Andalusian villages, farms and orchards, but she did not inquire about the name of the big city we passed, which led me

66

to believe she didn't know as much about Spain as I had thought.

However, like the girls, one more cathedral did not really hold much interest for me, even if it was considered one of Spain's treasures, so I pretended to be asleep as we passed.

My pretended slumber turned into the real thing during the remaining 70 mile drive to Seville. In fact, I didn't wake up until Pepe pulled up in front of a hotel that looked old but stately. Its big lobby, redundant with tiles and mahogany, had a typical Moorish motif that gave the feeling of ancient elegance.

By the time we were all settled in, it was after 9:00 P.M. and dusk had settled over the city so the view out my room's huge second floor window was pretty much confined to nearby rooftops, all of which---surprise---were composed of red tiles.

It occurred to me that I hadn't reported to Mr. Kimberly for a couple of days. Figuring in the seven hour difference in our times, it would be around two o'clock in the afternoon in Arizona so I used my cell phone to dial his cell phone number.

He answered right away, and I said, "Mr. Kimberly. It's me."

"Dorsey?" he said. "Hold on a second."

I heard footsteps and a door closing, so I assumed he was in his office and had closed the door. When he came back he said, "How's it going?"

"Good. We finished up in Madrid and we just arrived in Seville."

"Seville. Your second stop. Good." There was a brief pause before he asked, "Can you talk?"

I knew why he was asking. I said, "Yes. I'm in my room. Alone."

67

His voice dropped until it was almost a whisper. "What have you found out?"

I also spoke in a harsh whisper. "Nothing yet. Not a clue."

There was a brief pause. "Okay. Let me know as soon as you learn something. Anything."

"Okay. We're just going out to dinner. Maybe dancing afterward. If I find out..."

"Dinner? Dancing?" His voice climbed a little. "It has to be almost ten o'clock there."

By now I had settled in as a world traveler and I chuckled. "Over here we don't have dinner until at least ten, maybe eleven."

"Oh," he said. "Spain. Right. Well, keep at it. Call me the minute you find out anything about you know what."

"Yes, sir. But don't forget there is a time difference——-"

"Anytime. Day or night. Call me."

"Okay. Will do."

"Any time," he repeated and hung up.

I was thinking as I closed down my phone. I knew that learning the identity of the wealthy girl was important to him, but suppose I found out when it was about three o'clock in the morning his time. Would he still want me to wake him up in the middle of the night? Couldn't it wait until morning? Was it that important? Apparently so.

But one thing he hadn't figured. If I found out when it was about three in the morning here, Calvin Dorsey sure wasn't going to sacrifice his sleep to make the call. It couldn't be that important.

I checked my watch. Almost 10:00.

We had agreed to meet in the lobby at 10:00, and

although it was a little early for dinner in Spain, I figured the ladies would be pleased to hang out at some *tapas* bar.

In Madrid I had learned that almost every Spanish bar had *tapas* where one could load up on inexpensive appetizers before dinner, so I figured Seville would be loaded with good *tapas* bars. I proved to be right when the hotel's concierge directed us a place nearby he called a '*taperna*' that also served dinner even this early and had dancing after 10:30 P.M.

I guess the ladies' long nap during the ride from Madrid had restored their energy, because they were all raring to go. My own nap had been short, but I was feeling pretty good myself. Liza, as usual, seemed inexhaustible. During the short walk from the hotel to the bar, she laughed and skipped along as though she had slept throughout the trip, but I rather suspected her good humor was because her logistical preparations all seemed to be falling into place.

We arrived at the bar just as it was beginning to fill up so we were able to get a good table where the ladies ordered *Mahou* beer before they went over to the tapas counter and selected appetizers from the usual amazing variety. In addition to several kinds of cheese and fruit, this 'taperna' also offered clams simmered in garlic and grilled shrimp and stuffed crab and omelets and....well, you could pretty well ruin a good dinner by loading up with so many different appetizers they wouldn't all fit on the entire menu of most restaurants in Phoenix.

By the time the music started the ladies were all charged up with *tapas*, dinner and *Mahou*. At first the young men in the room were shy about asking the obvious foreign ladies to dance, and the girls started dancing with each other.

After one dance Maria sashaying her way back toward our table with her eyes on me, and I said to Liza, "Oh, Lordy I don't feel like dancing. I'm hiding under the table. Don't tell her."

Before I could make my move, Liza grabbed my arm. "No, you're not," she growled. "You've got to fill-in."

The musicians were whipping out a fast salsa, and I shook my head. "Not tonight. I'm beat."

Liza's stare told me otherwise as she said, "Doesn't matter. It's part of your job."

"It is?" Had I missed something when Mr. Kimberly had recruited me for the trip?

I guess I had because when Maria held out her arms and wiggled her fingers and other parts of her body at me, I suddenly didn't feel so tired, and my macho glands allowed her to entice me onto the dance floor.

But it wasn't for just one dance. I was expected to share my expertise with the other ladies, too.

I quickly discovered that Spanish musicians are indefatigable, and each dance seemed to go on forever. But thank heavens, after Heather and Dawn had also flung me around for about ten minutes, the local men began to move in, and I was able to collapse at our table

By this time Liza was dancing up a storm. In fact, she was as good as any of our girls, and even better than most of the Spanish girls, so I was a little surprised when after a few fast salsa numbers she came to the table and plopped down next to me. She wasn't even breathing hard.

I noticed she'd changed her drink from beer to

the sweet sherry which seemed to be the Spanish national drink.

"How's the sherry?" I asked. "Better than ours?"

"Depends," she said. "They have a greater variety. It's hard to get cream sherries at home, and I don't really care much for the dry kind." She nodded toward my cup of coffee. "How's the coffee?"

"Strong. You have to sip it. If you try to really drink it, it'll take your head off."

"You can always switch to sherry."

"I don't drink alcohol." I felt foolish saying it, but she might as well know.

She kind of gave me a sidelong look as though she wanted to ask me why, but she didn't say anything. I thought I'd better belay any misunderstanding she might have so I said, "I'm not an alcoholic. I just grew up in a family that doesn't drink."

She nodded. Maybe she was going to say something more but Dawn sashayed over to the table. "I need a man," she said, holding out her hands. "Come on, Calvin."

I didn't really feel like more dancing, but since it was apparently part of my job, I started to force myself to get up.

Liza put her hand on my shoulder. "We're talking," she said to Dawn. "Company business."

Dawn pouted her lovely lips. "Oh, poo," she said. Then she smiled at me. "Later, *guapa.*"

She wheeled away, her hips undulating to the salsa beat. I stared in her direction. *Guapa*? I knew that Spanish word. It meant 'handsome.' Wow.

I guess I kind of smiled because Liza quickly said, "It's a kind of dance. The *guapa.*"

I wondered if she knew she was wrong, or was

she simply jealous and didn't want me to know its real meaning. I choose to think it was the latter.

She quickly threw ice water on my inner glow by saying, "That's the sort of thing I mean. I want to talk to you about the ladies."

"The ladies?" From the tone of her voice whatever she was going to tell me would not be pleasant. I ran a quick search of my memory, looking for a clue that would lead me to what I had done wrong, and came up empty. Well, except for rubbing Dawn's feet. But that hadn't been my fault. I looked toward the dance floor. The ladies all appeared to be having a good time. Even Dawn had quickly snagged a partner. I girded up my loins for the worst and asked, "What about them?"

"It's alright to dance with them, like this. But I...uh...don't think you should get too...uh...close."

Close? With women who could probably have any man they wanted? Why would they choose me? On the other hand, maybe I really was *guapa*. Even so, as far as I was concerned the ladies were like sticks of dynamite that even a little body heat could result in my being blown to kingdom come. "Right," I said. "You're *la jefe*, the boss. I'm just a peon."

"It isn't that. But if there's ever a problem, I don't want anything to stand in the way when I have to fire you."

Well, if I harbored even a miniscule of attraction for any of the girls, what she'd said certainly put the final damper on even a subconscious ardor. I stared at her to see if she was serious. She stared back. Whoa! If she had hackles, they would be raised.

"Fire me?" I said. "I thought I was doing pretty well. If you're thinking about when I danced with

72

them, it was their idea. I didn't even ask for a waltz where I'd have to put my arms around--"

"I'm not talking about that." She continued to glare at me as though she had uncovered some inner Casanova I didn't even know I had.

"You're not?" I squeaked. I tried to match her glare, my mind continuing to race through events of the last few days. I had probably made a few little errors, but nothing that rated getting me fired.

"It's really not you," she said, and I relaxed a little. "It's them. I've seen the way they look at you. The way you look at them, even if you don't mean to. It's probably another innate masculine flaw. But if you cross the line, even a little bit, you're out."

Then I really did relax. There was no problem. I might be afflicted with some 'innate masculine flaw,' but the 'line' she was referring to might as well have been a stone wall.

Then I remembered what she'd said about the way they looked at me. "Don't give it a thought," I said with a devil-may-care smile. "They're just having fun. I don't take it seriously."

She wasn't buying it. "Look," she said. "I'm responsible for those girls. I've got problems enough on this tour. You don't know all the arrangements I have to deal with. I can't be worried about you, too. If you cause any trouble---and you know what I mean by 'trouble'---I'll see that you spend the rest of your life in jail...a Spanish jail. Is that clear?"

I failed to see how it could be any clearer. She had hacked into my mind with words that were like viruses, words that attack the part of my mental hard drive that was my conscious. If I had been harboring any romantic thoughts---even subconscious romantic

73

thoughts---about the four girls, or any girl within a hundred miles, the idea of spending time in a Spanish dungeon erased them from my mind, even my primitive ego-libido mind. In fact, especially my ego-libido mind. Still, I had to let Liza know my position.

"But if they ask me to dance or something, like Dawn just did, I can't very well say no."

"I'm not talking about dancing, things like that. I'm talking about those 'or somethings.' You know what I'm talking about."

I may sometimes appear naive, but I understood what she meant: don't fall in love with any of them, and make sure none of them fell in love with me. I may be 'guapa' but I wasn't 'stupido.' The idea that one of them...or, heaven forbid...all of them would be attracted to me was flattering. But it was also laughable. I might be acceptable as a fill-in during emergencies, but I was not so naïve as to believe that they would fall in love with me, especially since one of them could have any man in the world she wanted.

I was about to tell Liza, "Ha. I'm not that lucky" when I suddenly had a brilliant idea. One of the girls was so rich she could, indeed, get any man she wanted, so she certainly wouldn't be interested in little old Calvin Dorsey. All I had to do was make each of them fall in love with me. The one who was able to resist would have to be the golden girl. Voila! Problem solved.

I grinned at Liza. Solving this problem was going to be real fun. There was just one little glitch.

Judging by the look in Liza's eyes, it could also get me killed, or worse, thrown in a Spanish calaboose. I knew I could keep my own amorous machinations a secret, but could they? Obviously, each of the girls was

74

definitely danger incarnate, and I would be risking my life by breaking their hearts, even if I really was '*guapa.*'

On the other hand....

CHAPTER 6

As it turned out, it wasn't fraternizing with the girls that threatened to cut short my future. Later that night, when I walked into my hotel room and reached for the light switch, a raspy voice said, "No. Don't touch the light."

I knew that voice. The skinny paparazzi guy.

A sudden charge of anger grabbed me. Who the devil was this guy to give me orders. I said, "Go to hell," and reached for the light switch.

Before I could touch it a hand the size of a baseball glove grabbed my arm, and the rumbling voice of the burly guy said, "No lights. Right, Simon?"

The skinny guy snarled, "I told you, Bruno. No names, you dumb ox."

Bruno said, "Oh yeah. Right."

He twisted my arm harder. "No lights."

The way he gripped my arm I couldn't have reached the light switch with a bulldozer, so I said, "Okay. No lights."

He said, "Good," and gave me a shove that catapulted me across the room and slammed me into the bed where I ended up sitting on the edge. There was enough illumination coming in around the window curtain from outside patio lights so I could make out the big guy standing between me and the door and the skinny one sitting across the room on a couch. I would not have been surprised to see a gun in his hand.

"You're wasting your time," I said. "I haven't any money."

"Who said anything about money?" Simon said. "We want to give you money, not take it."

76

"Give me money?" Now there was a switch.

"A business deal," he said. "Strictly business."

I looked at Bruno standing in front of the door. "You mean a deal I can't refuse?"

The skinny guy's face was in shadow, but I could sense his smile. "This ain't Chicago," he said. "You give us a little cooperation and we give you a few hundred bucks. That's a legit business deal."

I knew I was never going to engage in a business deal with these guys no matter what it was, but I thought it prudent not to tell them, at least, not immediately. I considered starting a fight. We would make so much noise the guys would have to split. On the other hand, I would probably end up in a hospital, which did not seem practical. Besides, I kind of wondered what it was they wanted so badly they were willing to pay for it.

Oh, wait. Of course. The Cinderella girl.

To confirm my suspicion, Simon said, "Just tell me which one she is. That's all. No big deal."

"What are you talking about?" I said. "Tell you what?"

"Look," he said. "We only want a couple of pictures. Which one is she?"

Pictures? This might be my chance to learn something. "Why do you want pictures of some girl? Who would want them?"

He got up and walked the couple of feet to stand in front of me. Out of the shadows where I could see every feature of his long, thin face, he looked even more menacing. "They didn't tell you?" he said.

I was also able to see that when he spoke he kind of pulled his upper lip up in a grim kind of sneer. It was intimidating enough so that I put on my most guileless expression and said, "Tell me what?"

He stood staring at me for a second, then turned to the big guy. "What do you think, Bruno? Is he lying?"

Bruno's said, "I don't know, Simon. Want me to ask him?" His evil smile when he said it was enough to make me want to confess to something, anything.

He took a step toward me, and I blurted to the skinny guy. "Wait! Wait! I confess. I'm the one. I did it."

He blinked and his mouth dropped open. "Huh?" he said. "Did what?"

"Anything," I said. "I confess. It was my fault. I did it."

The skinny guy---what was his name? Oh, yeah. Simon---jerked his head at Bruno. "Enough with the games," he said. "Do it."

Bruno sort of chuckled and curled his big hands into fists the size of sledge hammers. It's amazing how terror can increase one's speed. Before he took even one step I had already darted across the room and wrenched the door open.

"Hey," Bruno said. "Where you goin'?"

"Find a priest," I yelped. "To confess."

Bruno and the skinny guy were staring at each other when I rushed out and slammed the door behind me. I didn't hurry too much as I went down the hotel's wide stairway leading to the lobby. I knew that out here in the open they could never catch me. They undoubtedly knew this too, and if they were smart they would be leaving by the same exit they'd entered.

Taking a seat in the hotel lobby where I could watch the ancient elevator and the stairs, I gave them plenty of time to sneak out, which I'm sure they would.

78

There would be no point in their waiting. I certainly would not be returning while there was a chance they would still be there.

The wait also gave me time to think: they might only be paparazzi, but how had they learned about one of the girls being a billion heiress? And were they really paparazzi or were they after more than pictures? Should I warn Liza? If I did she'd want to know why they wanted pictures of one of the girls, and I'd have to let her in on the secret. But if the goons gave up on me and went after her, would they believe it when she said she had no idea what they were talking about, or would that guy Simon refuse to take ignorance for an answer? Maybe I should tell her.

On the other hand, she had enough to worry about. Knowing that one of the girls was hazardous for everybody would only add to her problems. On the other hand.....

Thinking about it while I worked up the nerve to return to my room did not provide any logical answers.

When I got there, my room was, of course, deserted. I locked the door, even though the ancient lock hadn't deterred them before. I finally made it to bed, after barricading the door with a chair. I thought maybe sleep would bring some answers. I was wrong. I tossed and turned until I finally drifted off, but the only things that came to my mind were nightmares, all of them featuring Bruno's evil smile.

CHAPTER 7

I think Seville should be known as the city of church bells, because it was the incessant tolling of bells that eventually forced me out of bed the next morning at about 11:00 A.M. When I saw the four girls, it was difficult to remember Liza's admonitions about not even thinking about romancing them. Despite the late hour last night and all the dancing, they looked gorgeous, with rapturous hair,(well, all except Dawn, of course) beautiful faces, breathtaking figures clad in the latest fashions of blouses, long tights or trousers and miniskirts or dresses. Even Liza looked fresh and eager for adventure. But with my extraordinary willpower, I was able to appear all business when we met for our noon brunch before we began taking in the sights of Seville.

I knew I couldn't keep up my charade of being bright-eyed and bushy-tailed for long. I was sure my eyes must look like two half-open clam shells. I was also sure that none of the ladies had been plagued by nightmares about Bruno. When they saw me and my bleary eyes they gave me those looks of disapproval that only females can conjure up. I told them there had been a pea under my mattress. Then they really did look at me as though I were demented.

But after we started our trek I was so struck by the beauty of Seville, it didn't take me long to come alive.

With Pepe driving we started at the famous Plaza de España. Its tile paving of colorful mosaics as well as the surrounding picturesque buildings whose arabesque mosaics reflected the Moor's 300 year reign.

80

I was especially fascinated by a bridge with blue and white railings made of some material that looked like ceramic and with elaborate support columns crowned with tall, ornate blue and white ceramic vases.

The entire plaza was such a dazzling work of art that even the ladies seemed to enjoy examining the artistic designs in its many famous murals.

Then it was off to visit Seville's most distinctive landmark: the imposing *Santa Maria de la Sede cathedral.* Despite the girls' seeming aversion to cathedrals, they couldn't help but be awed by this one. Before we went inside, I surreptitiously consulted my tour book so that I was able to amaze the ladies with my knowledge. For instance, I was able to explain that the *Santa Maria de la Sede*, like many of the Spanish cathedrals, was build over the remnants of an ancient Moorish mosque. I got a few "ohs" and "ahs," when I pointed out that the Roman Catholic church took more than a hundred years to complete and is so huge that only St. Peter's in Rome is bigger.

Its bell tower, known as *La Giralda*, is one of the tallest structures in Seville. Not surprising none of the ladies felt like trudging up the winding ramp to the top no matter how magnificent the view would be.

To my surprise and delight, after I managed to herd them inside the ancient cathedral and pointed out several masterpieces of art, they actually asked questions about the artists and I was able to expound on such renowned masters as Goya and Murillo. When we looked at the cathedral's alter piece and I told them it was the largest in the world, they still weren't too impressed until and I pointed out how it was decorated with the meticulously carved figures of more than a thousand biblical characters. Then I think they, too, marveled at the genius and the hard work that had produced it.

The mood of the moment seemed to hold while I led them next door to the beautiful filigreed royal palace known as the *Seville Alcãzar.* Built almost a thousand years ago by the Moors, the *Alcãzar* was originally a fortress before it was converted to a palace for Spanish royalty.

I don't know about the ladies, but during our tour, I was fascinated at how the facts I'd read were brought to life by our observations. They sort of got the idea, however, when, walking through the so called 'Courtyard of the Maidens,' I recalled that the courtyard got its name from the legend that every year the old Moorish rulers demanded that the Christians contribute one-hundred virgins to them. They were disappointed when I told them the legend was nothing but a story. Actually, I was a little disappointed myself because, looking at the ancient Moorish walls and gardens, I wondered how many other falsehoods they could have absorbed over the centuries.

In addition to an attempt to instill some respect for history in the ladies' heads, I had an ulterior motive for introducing them to such marvels. As we toured the city, I watched each one carefully, looking for some clue that would tell me which of them had probably attended the most prestigious universities in the world and, therefore, should exhibit some appreciation of the history that was unfolding before their eyes. But no. None of the four girls seemed more impressed, more curious, than the others.

The few times they did asked questions I was able to answer most of them without too much imaginative embellishment. But no matter how much amazing knowledge and enthusiasm I put into my dissertations, the girls seemed more interested in the shops we passed and what the native men looked like than anything I said, no matter how profound. Unfortunately, neither the shops nor the men looked as ancient as I would have liked.

Their interest perked up, however, when I mentioned that the famous Don Juan used to live in Seville. When I told them he was supposed to have **seduced more than** a thousand **Spanish maidens**, that got their attention.

"A thousand?" Maria said. "Were they all virgins?"

"I don't know," I said. "But a thousand? I don't see how he found time to eat and sleep."

"What about you?" Dawn said. "How many have you seduced?"

I felt my face turn red, but I quickly said, "In Nevada? There are no virgins."

They laughed and when they saw the color of my face they would have pursued the subject but Liza, who had been using her cell phone, pulled me aside.

"We've got a problem," she said.

"We?" I looked toward the girls who were still discussing Don Juan. "I don't have a problem."

"Yes, you do. Tonight we're scheduled to see that flamenco dancer Don Miguel."

"At the famous Alegoria. I remember. It's in our itinerary. One of the original flamenco places."

"I just found out: he's sick. He can't make it. They've cancelled the show."

"Oh, when will he be back?"

"It doesn't matter. We have to leave tomorrow."

"So, we go somewhere else. Seville is the home

of flamenco. There are clubs all over the place. What's the problem?"

"The problem is it's in our contract: The one-and-only Don Miguel at the Alegoria. They could sue us."

I stared at her. Who would put such a nebulous thing in a tour contract? I mean, people do get sick, even famous people. Then I remembered that the father of one of the toures was a billionaire. I guess he could put anything he wanted in a contract.

Suddenly, I had a brilliant idea. "Hey. We get another dancer. Our girls have never been here. They wouldn't know one guy from another."

"My idea exactly," she said. "Except it's impossible to find somebody available who can do flamenco on short notice."

I shook my head in disbelief. "In Seville? There's got to be somebody."

She nodded. "There is." She gave me a look that froze my blood before she said, "You."

It was as though she had smashed a fist into my solar plexus. I stumbled back a couple of steps. "Oh, no. Not me. I don't do flamenco. I don't even know any flamencos."

"Why not? You said it yourself: they wouldn't know one guy from another."

"But they'll know me!"

"Not if you're in costume, with a mustache, one of those Gypsy hats, a little makeup."

My brain reeled, searching for a way out. "But they'll know when I start to dance. I can't do flamenco. I can just barely get by in a waltz."

"Of course you can. Just stomp your feet and wave your hands over your head. The Señoritas, the

84

back-up dancers, can do the hard stuff."

I shook my head. "No, no. It's not that simple—
"

"Yes, it is." She closed the gap between us, grabbing the front of my shirt. "You've got to do it. There's nobody else."

"No," I couldn't even imagine being on that stage, a stage where some of the greatest flamenco dancers in the world had performed. "I won't make a fool of myself. I won't do it."

I tried to pry her hands loose from my shirt, but she had a grip like a crocodile's bite. "Yes, you will," she said. "It's in your contract."

That froze me. I had to struggle to keep an ugly darkness from clouding my brain. I managed to say, "It is? How did they know this was going to happen?"

"It's a catch-all clause. Like dancing with the girls."

I suddenly lost all my strength, giving up on trying to pry away her hands. "Catch-all?"

"In essence it says you're to give necessary aide to the tour manager---that's me---when it's required. Like now."

I slowly shook my head. "No, no. I checked my contract. It's says I'm a tour guide. Period."

She let go of my shirt. "Check again. That's not a period. It's a coma."

The black cloud got blacker. "It is?"

"It's in the fine print. Did you read the fine print?"

I shook my head. "It was too small."

"So now you know why it's so small."

"But..." I searched frantically for a ray of light in the darkness. "I'm sick. The same thing as Don

85

Miguel. It hits all of us flamenco dancers."

"Good idea," she said. "I'll tell the girls you're not with us because you're sick."

"Does that mean I don't have to do it?"

She wasn't listening. "Right now, stay here with the girls. Finish the tour. I'll go find you a costume."

"But..." I stopped. I was all out of 'buts.' Besides, she had already gone.

The remainder of the day was a blur. I don't know who was more relieved when I cut it short: me or the girls.

After we returned to the hotel, I dug out my guide book and tried to find something---anything---on flamenco dancing. There was nothing. I was on my own, just me and my big feet. I really was sick.

CHAPTER 8

I'd read somewhere in the past when I was happy and innocent that flamenco dancing had been invented by Gypsies, and that Seville is the home of authentic flamenco. The most famous venues are often dark, smoky places where the music, provided by a single guitarist, always seems to be a heartbreaking lament. The dancing itself, however, with each dance telling a story filled with pain and sorrow, is spirited with much arm and foot movement. There is some tap dancing involved, but flamenco seems to be more foot-and-heel stomping than tap dancing. The music, no matter how soul twisting, has a distinctive beat that the women dancers often augment with clicking castanets.

I had no idea where Liza located my flamenco dancer's costume, but when she did she should have taken me with her because her guess at my size could have used some of my input. It seemed like most male flamenco dancers are less than six feet tall and weigh about as much as a racehorse jockey. The white shirt and black jacket she gave me, although a little tight, weren't such a bad fit, but trying to squeeze into the tight pants required the use of words I was surprised I even knew. The shoes, with two-inch heels, impossible. I wear size twelve and flamenco dancers all wear size six or smaller. I finally gave up on the shoes and just wore my own brogans.

Liza topped it off by making my hair coal black with a dye she said would wash off. Then she used makeup to darken my complexion before she painted on a thin mustache that curled up at the ends.

But it was the hat that turned the tide. I loved it.

87

Black, with a flat top and wide, flat brim and with a red string that tied under my chin. Wearing it kind of tipped forward to shield my piercing eyes, I even felt like a macho dancer. Checking myself in a mirror, I was amazed at how good I looked. I should wear this getup all the time. No wonder Don Juan seduced a thousand virgins. He must have dressed like a flamenco dancer, especially with the mustache and hat. I pulled my shoulders back, arched my arms over my head and curled my lips in a sneer. I even felt like a dancer.

That is until I found myself waiting in the wings of the stage listening to the solo guitar player while two authentic female flamenco dancers performed, knowing that in a couple of minutes, as the lone male dancer, I would be exposed as a fake.

Watching the female dancers cavorting around the stage, clicking castanets, stamping their feet and using their arms and hands with hypnotic grace, I wished that male dancers also used castanets because their clicks would help cover up my inept hand and foot movements.

There was also the disparaging difference in costumes. The two ladies, clad in traditional colorful dresses with skirts full enough to hide a blimp and with their shoulders and upper arms concealed by massive ruffles, could simply whirl or shake their skirts, stomp their feet, writhe their arms over their heads while clicking away with their castanets and everyone thought they were watching authentic flamenco.

They also had the advantage of seductive eyes, and black, black hair decorated with red flowers, and with beautiful faces so heavily made up they could range in age from teen to octogenarian and no one could tell the difference.

One cardinal rule I did learn from my guide book about flamenco: a dancer must never, never, never ever smile. Flamenco is a dance of pain and sorrow. To look as though you were enjoying the music and the dance would mean that your heart was not breaking, and if authentic flamenco was based upon one thing it was pure heartbreaking, tear-jerking pathos.

Well, in my mood that part was **going to be easy**. When my cue came I knew I would already be crying. And as soon as the audience saw my attempt to mimic a flamenco dancer, they would be crying, too.

Suddenly, the two ladies on the stage shook out their skirts, twirled a couple of times, clicked their castanets furiously, stomped their feet, shouted "Ole!" and headed for the wings on the other side of the stage, where they stood, just off stage, staring suspiciously across the stage at me.

I still might have escaped, but Liza was right behind me. She said, "Get ready," and put her hand in the small of my back.

I said, "Can I take another look at that contract."

She said, "No. Here put this in your mouth."

I opened my mouth to say "Huh" and she slapped a rose stem between my teeth.

I gave a muffled "Ow." She'd forgotten to remove the thorns.

Too late.

The guitar player---who sat on a folding chair off to the side of the stage---banged out a chord, zipped through a fantastic arpeggio, and launched into my cue.

"Go!" Liza said.

I shook my head. "Uh uh."

She shoved, hard.

I went. By the time I regained my balance, I was in the center of the stage and everybody in the audience was applauding and yelling 'Oley.' Since there was only four of them they didn't make much noise.

But it was enough. I was hung out to dry!

With no choice, I threw out my chest, waved my hands over my head and stomped my feet. Hey! I was doing it. My shoes, with no long pants to hide their size, looked like boats, but I managed to whip them into a syncopated thumping with the beat of the music that brought a round of applause from the four girls and a couple of waitresses.

With perfect rhythm, I stomped away, clapped my hands over my head and grimacing like my heart was breaking. I was just getting into it, when the music twanged to a stop as though the guitar player had suddenly realized I wasn't the real Don Miguel. I gave a couple of leaping stomps and bowed.

The ladies applauded even louder and I heard one of them say, "Calvin? Is that Calvin."

Another said, "No. He's sick." Which was the excuse Liza had given them to account for my being a no-show.

I was about to bow my way off stage when the guitarist started banging away at another song as though to force me into action. I had no choice. Besides, I was getting the hang of it.

I straightened, waved my arms above my head, twirled my hands, and began stomping my feet in a cadence that would have made any flamenco dancer envious.

If I do say so myself, I think I did pretty well. At first my mind was more on keeping my pants from splitting than on my dancing, but once I got the rhythm and began to make the moves I'd seen flamenco dancers perform in movies, I thought I was pretty good. After all, it was the guitar player's job to keep in sync with my foot stomping not the other way around. Wasn't it?

Cavorting around the small stage, stomping my feet, snapping my fingers and clapping my hands over my head like castanets, I discovered that if I stomped hard enough I could actually raise dust from the ancient floor.

I almost smiled. I'll bet no other flamenco foot-pounder could do that!

I think the high point of my dance came when I plucked the rose from my teeth, leaped in the air in a giant mazurka, and tossed the rose to the girls.

Unfortunately, my performance came to a rather ignominious end when, at that point, someone started taking flash pictures. I thought it was one of the ladies until I noticed the flashes came from the wings of the stage and instead of being directed at me, were directed at the four ladies.

I stomped my way over to the side of the stage and saw Bruno and Simon, the paparazzi guys. The skinny guy, Simon, had a camera and, sure enough, was taking pictures of the girls!

I said, "Hey!" and leaped at him, knocking the camera from his hand. I saw it bounce off the apron of the stage just as Bruno grabbed me and flung me back across the stage.

In a way it was more fortunate than unfortunate

when I slammed into the guitar player and put him and his guitar out of action. He added to the drama with a shrill scream, which, one could say, effectively ended my performance on a high note.

Regaining my balance I charged back across the stage to do battle with the two goons. I was startled to find Liza right beside me.

Too late. They were gone, probably out some backstage door.

When we couldn't locate them, Liza hissed, "Go, before the girls see you. Meet us back at the hotel."

I took the cue and ran past the two startled female flamenco dancers, back through the dressing rooms, where I grabbed the raincoat I'd worn over my costume when I came in, and hustled out a side door.

I ran around to the street in front of the theatre, arriving in time to see a small, yellow car zooming away.

The rest of the evening, after I'd washed off the makeup and changed my clothes---I hated to give up the hat, and the mustache looked definitely cool---and I'd made a miraculous recover from my 'illness,' we all spent the next few hours sampling the music and the *tapas* in half the *tapa* bars of Seville (and that's a <u>lot</u> of *tapa*). The ladies all had a good laugh telling me about the inept flamenco dancer before some crazy paparazzi had ruined the show. But I didn't do much laughing. For one thing, I didn't think I'd been that bad. For another, I wondered how those paparazzi had found us. At least now I was pretty sure why they were taking pictures of the girls: somehow they knew that one of them was the daughter of one of the richest men in the world. But apparently, they also didn't know which one.

I wondered how they had found out she was one of the bevy? One good thing: we had found their camera at the foot of the stage, so they had no pictures.

Throughout the evening, as we went from bar to bar, Liza was unusually subdued, and I wondered what she was thinking. Mr. Kimberly said she wasn't in on the secret that one of the girls was mega-rich. But she had to wonder why the paparazzi had followed us all the way from Madrid. She had to be suspicious that it **was not just because they were** four ordinary **American** girls. Well, maybe they weren't 'ordinary' but they certainly weren't worthy of being singled out from all the American girls touring Spain.

I, of course, knew why. It had to be they were trying to get pictures of the four girls with the hope that later someone would be able to identify the golden princess. What other reason could there be? Could I be wrong? Perhaps there was a big market in fashion magazines of four lovely American girls traveling in a foreign country. Maybe it wasn't the girls at all. Maybe it was what they were wearing.

I hoped that was the case, but I had a sneaking suspicion that it was not. Somehow those two goons had found out the secret. Or they thought they had.

But whatever their motives, it seemed as though it had become my job to protect the girls. Thinking about the size of Bruno and the menace in the eyes of the skinny one, I really didn't want the responsibility. If I were the only line of defense, the girls really were in danger. But what choice did I have? I could quit, of course. Simply walk away. But, as the girls' only chaperon, that would leave Liza in danger with no clue about why.

Thinking of Liza, I just hoped she never found

93

out about the golden girl. Especially since I had a question of more immediate importance nagging at me: how did she like my dance? I was afraid to ask.

CHAPTER 9

As usual lately, it was almost four o'clock in the morning before I was able to get ready for bed. I was dead tired as much from the mental anguish of preparing for the flamenco as by the dance itself. Plus I now had to worry about the two paparazzi goons. Then my weary body and churning mind had not been helped by the long evening of traipsing from *tapas* bar to *tapas* bar, each with its inexhaustible cadre of musicians and five women who would rather dance than sit and talk.

I had put on my pajamas and started to crawl into bed when I heard a soft knock. At first I thought it was a knock on the wall, and I muttered a couple of bad Spanish words I'd picked up. But the knock sounded again, and I realized it was a knock on my door.

My room was actually a large bedroom furnished with a king-sized bed, a couch behind a small coffee table, a couple of wooden chairs, and a big dresser with a mirror. The small bathroom had a tiny closet and a tub with a shower.

It was only a few steps from the bed to the entrance door, but the walk gave me enough time for images about who might be outside the door to flash through my mind. One thing was certain: it couldn't be Simon and Bruno. They would never gently knock on the door. They would have broken it down.

So who was it? The hotel concierge? With some bad news that couldn't wait until morning? Gypsy flamenco dancers, here to kill me for what I had done to their dance? The guitarist? Here to kill me for what I had done to his guitar? One of the four girls? Who could get me thrown in a Spanish prison? Dawn maybe? Had I done too good a job of foot-rubbing?

None of the suppositions promised to be in my best interest, so when I eased the door open a crack, I was ready for fight or flight. At first the hall light was so dim I had trouble recognizing who it was, and when I did, I discovered I'd been holding my breath and it sort of gushed out in relief. Liza.

My trepidation immediately changed from the fear of being badly mutilated by some irate Gypsy to the fear of someone seeing Liza in front of my door in the dead of night, and I almost pulled her inside and closed the door.

"What is it?" I said. "Is something wrong?"

Stupid question. Of course something was wrong. Why else would she be knocking on my door?

My fears were realized when she said, "We've got to talk."

Now? When a woman says 'we've got to talk' whatever it is she wants to talk about will always be unpleasant. So I steeled myself for the worst as I turned on every light I could find, then moved a chair into the middle of the room for her while I perched on the edge of the bed, and waited for the sword to fall.

She didn't begin right away, as though reluctant to release the bad news, and I had time to noticed that with her hair tumbling down, framing her face, and even with no makeup, and for once looking more worried than annoyed, she was surprisingly lovely. The rest of her also looked above average. Instead of her usual serviceable shoes, she wore slippers made of some kind of faux fur with good-sized heels. Her terrycloth robe was disconcertingly open in front over

96

what looked like a satin nightgown that clung to her as though it wanted to protect her from my burning gaze. Could she be naked under the nightgown? My idiot mind, although fraught with worry about her late night visit, still managed to wonder if it was all she wore.

My anxiety lost a battle with my rampaging imagination. Liza, coming to my bedroom in the middle of the night with her lustrous hair down and wearing almost no clothes? What could be bad about that?

I found out when she snapped me back to reality by saying, "Those two men? Who are they? Why are they following us?"

Well, so much for romance.

"I have no idea," I said. "I never saw them before that time at the airport."

"If they're paparazzi, what do they want with us? We're nobody."

"Nobodies," I corrected. "The plural of nobody."

She sort of grimaced with consternation as though deliberately trying to avoid my astute observation. "You know what I mean," she said but without her usual tone of irk.

"Well, yes. What I mean is you're right. Why do they want our pictures? And following us all the way to Seville? It doesn't make sense."

I hoped the note of concern in my voice would keep her from guessing what I was really thinking: how did the men know about the princess and, of more importance, how is it they always seemed to know where we would be? Their motives were easy to guess. Somehow they knew about the golden girl. And I'm sure that a picture of her---if they could positively identify her---would be worth a fortune.

"They must have us mixed up with some other group," she said, more to herself than to me. "Like some rock band."

I kind of sighed with relief. She didn't know either. "I think you're right. Maybe I should have a talk with them, if they're still around."

She gave me a look that was filled with more skepticism than confidence as though if I did find the two men I might end up impaled on the short end of the stick. Still, she said, "Good idea. Tell them to leave us alone."

She began moving toward the door, and while I really didn't want her to leave, I was more than a little concerned that she would guess what I was thinking, which was how great she would look if she could work up a smile.

It seemed that she knew my mind better than I did because she glanced at my face and instinctively pulled the top of her robe closed. A surge of satisfaction lifted my ego. Once again I was right; women always know when a man is thinking about sex even when he might not know it himself. Other times they believed he is not thinking at all. I'd just have to control my subconscious, or I would be the one in trouble.

"See you in the morning," she said and left, leaving a faint trail of perfume that would have allowed her to read my mind the rest of the night if she had hung around.

98

CHAPTER 10

The next morning...actually, the next early afternoon...we bundled into Pepe's SUV and set off for our next destination: a little town called Ronda.

I'd looked the place up on my map and discovered it wasn't that far from Seville, about fifty miles southeast toward the Costa del Sol, where **Andalusia** borders the **Mediterranean**.

At first the wide highway, stretching across rolling Andalusia plains, was easy going until we reached a place called Antequera where Pepe swung off onto a narrow highway that wound through low-lying rugged mountains.

After being surrounded by the fields and orchards of Andalusia for the last couple of days, I rather enjoyed the mountains and arroyos for a change. But the four girls did not, since zipping around the endless curves made it difficult to sleep.

When one of the girls, Maria, awakened by a sharp bend, stared out the window at the brush-covered hills, she said, "Hey. This doesn't look like Spain."

"Southern Andalusia, the real Spain," Liza told her. "One of the oldest parts. These hills have known Stone Age people, Romans, Visigoths, Moors, Christians, everything. Ronda, where we're going, is one of the oldest cities in Spain, and one of the most picturesque. Tell them, Calvin."

Tell them what? She had already told them everything I knew. "Oh, yeah, sure." I tried to remember what I had tried to memorize about the city of Ronda. "As Liza said, it's a very old city. Old castles.

Old cathedrals---"

"Oh God. Not another cathedral," Heather said.

"There's always a cathedral," I answered. "But this time it isn't the most important part of the city. What makes Ronda unique is that it's...uh...what? Oh, yeah...split in half by a deep gorge, narrow but really deep."

"Deeper than Grand Canyon?" Dawn said with a yawn. "I've seen Grand Canyon."

"It's not quite Grand Canyon. And the streets are all really old and...uh...narrow."

Valerie said, "Why build a city in such a lousy place?"

"Probably because it was easy to defend against invaders. Makes it very colorful. Some people say it's the most picturesque city in Spain."

"Does it have *tapas*?" Valerie continued.

Pepe interjected: "Every place in Spain have *tapas*."

"Good," Valerie said, and closed her eyes.

"If it's so old," Marie said, "why are we going there?"

I looked at Liza. "Yeah. Why are we going there?"

"Bull fights," she said. "Ronda has the oldest bullring in Spain. They're having a celebration with a series of bull fights. All the famous bullfighters will be there."

"Oh," The mention of bullfighters brought Heather wide awake. "I love bullfighters."

"Me, too," Dawn said. "They're so macho."

I'd never seen a bullfight, except in the movies, but I thought that Dawn had to be right. With only the thin cloth of a cape between you and two sharply

100

pointed horns trying to spear you, being a bullfighter would take a lot of machismo. I was glad it was the kind of courage I'd never have to experience.

Like a fool, I thought too soon.

I was still enjoying the scenery in ignorant bliss when we entered the small legendary city and Pepe took us on a little tour before driving to the hotel.

Crossing one of the three bridges spanning the narrow gorge created by the Tajo River that divided the town, we all stared down in awe at the dancing waters of the river more than 300 feet below.

"This is the bridge most *antiego*," Pepe said. "Made by the Romans, I think, more than a thousand years ago."

Telling the girls that the only thing separating them from the water far below was a thousand-year old stone bridge, did not inspire confidence.

Maria sucked in air between her clinched teeth. "Can we go a little faster?"

"Yes," Heather chipped in. "I think this thing is crumbling."

Pepe laughed and continued across the bridge. I hoped no one had noticed that I had been gripping the front edge of my seat so hard my knuckles had turned white.

But I kept smiling and, after all, that's what counts when you want to prove your machismo.

My smile, however, did not last long.

That evening we discovered that for a small town with much of it perched on the edge of a precipice, Ronda supported a surprising number of *tapas* bars that like all Spanish bars, had no closing time, so as usual lately, it was around 4:00 A.M. when I crawled into bed.

101

This time when the knob on the door rattled, followed by a soft knock, I took my time dragging my body out of bed and switching on a lamp while thinking about a quote I'd read somewhere: 'A body at rest wants to stay at rest; a body in motion wants to go back to bed.'

Parts of my body changed their mind about being at rest when I opened the door in the middle of a yawn and saw that my visitor was not Liza. It was Valerie. Valerie, with her glistening mass of red hair and her awesome, long legs sticking out of a brief pajama top and her wide hazel eyes not showing even a hint of being sleepy.

It's amazing how quickly one's mind can leap from thoughts about problems with paparazzi to the wonders of a lovely girl wearing only a pajama top to the terror of being drawn and quartered in a Spanish jail.

Still, like a fool, I opened the door. "Valerie," I said. "What is it? Something wrong?"

She quickly glanced up and down the dimly lit hall before she kind of whispered, "I've got this sore foot. Would you look at it?"

My revengeful mind must have harbored a secret desire to see me in a Spanish dungeon because I heard my mouth say, "Uh, sure. Come in."

When she slipped passed me the scent of some exotic perfume sent my mind reeling and, stupid me, I closed the door.

Before I could even turn around Valerie had turned off the lamp and thrown herself on my bed. My bed? There was enough moonlight filtering through the curtains of a window to see her reclining on one elbow, smiling. Oh, Lordy, Lordy.

I kind of sidled toward the foot of the bed where her long naked legs ended and croaked, "A chair. Could you sit in a chair?"

She frowned, making me wonder how she could make even a frown sexy.

"I don't think so. Chairs hurt my foot."

Instead of asking how that was possible, I said. "Oh." And my own feet dragged me close to the bed where I stood mesmerized by her lovely, but obviously painful, feet. "Uh...wha...which foot?"

She wriggled her toes. "Both. My knees, too."

I was going to sit on the end of the bed, but thought better of it and knelt on the floor in front of her sexy legs where it took an amazing amount of stupidity to say, "I only do feet."

"Oh," I could tell by the sound of her voice that her adorable, luscious lips were in a pretend pout. "Do you do backs?" she kind of breathed.

Backs? Lovely, smooth backs covered with soft, warm skin that went all the way down to... Oh, Lordy, Lordy. "Feet," I said. "I only do feet."

I grabbed one foot and began a quick massage.

"Uoooo. Easy," she said. "Not so hard."

I sort of got control of my hands and eased up on the message. It only took about two seconds before my fingers began to enjoying their work. I'd never though much about how really sexy feet can be---my own especially---but when Valarie began making little mewing sounds as I caressed her plantar arch, I had serious thoughts of becoming a podiatrist.

I was beginning to wonder if I should go to work on her poor sore knees, when my mind reminded me that this was my chance to find out if she were the golden girl.

I considered asking her directly, but that would probably be counterproductive. Since she was intent on concealing her true identity, she would not truthfully answer a direct question. And if she wasn't the chosen one, my question would raise questions.

So I playing detective by circling the big question while I delicately traced suggestive circles on her metatarsal, beginning with, "Where you from?"

"What?" she said. "Who cares? Do the other foot."

"Yeah, okay. Just curious. I understand you're matriculating at some university."

"Matriculating?" She lifted her head and chuckled. "Oh, yes. I love to matriculate. I can tell by your touch that you do, too."

Uh, oh. "Me? Matriculate?" She obviously misunderstood the meaning of the word. "No, no," I hastily said. "I've never matriculated. I just do feet. No knees. Only feets. Foots. Never knees."

"Oh? Never? Okay. Do my back."

She rolled over onto her stomach and pulled her pajama top up. Thank heavens she was wearing panties.

As I crawled around to the side of the bed so I could reach her back, I asked. "What's your major at the university?"

"Law," she said.

Law? Did that mean she was aiming for politics? Maybe with her eye on becoming president.

"What kind? Corporate? Trust funds? Hedge funds?"

"Criminal law, mostly," she said. "I'd like to be a public defender some day."

"Help the poor. I like that."

"Good. And if you ask any more questions I'm going to sue you."

That slowed me down, but it didn't stop me. I refused to be intimidated. Not Calvin Dorsey. Still, kneeling beside the bed, I began working on her back, and instantly forgot what I was going to ask her.

I kept enough of my senses to confine my rubbing to an area up around her neck. But then she said, "A little lower. I think it's my hip."

I paused, my hands hovering in midair while my brain fought my libido. Go, go, my libido demanded. Lower, lower. But my brain's neocortex said, "Are you crazy? You'll end up in jail for the rest of your life." And, with my eyes staring at Valerie's perfect derriere, my evil libido answered, "It'll be worth it."

Outclassed, my noble neocortex was about to lose the one-sided battle when there was a soft knock on the door. My brain shouted in triumph. "Police. I told you, *stupido.* You're going to jail!"

I struggled to my feet trying to think of a place to hide. If the police did not see me, they might think this was Valarie's room.

I was heading for the closet when Valerie sat up, saying, "What is this? Have you got another girl?"

I didn't want the police to hear my voice so I didn't answer. But Valerie's question was answered when the door---that I forgotten to lock---swung open and another girl came in.

I stopped so fast I almost fell. Heather, her blonde hair curling down over her magnificent chest, her long legs mesmerizing below a short pajama top, her luscious lips parted in surprise as her startled blue eyes focused on the girl on my bed.

"Val," she said. "What are you doing here?"

Valerie put her legs over the side of he bed and wiggled her toes. "Sore foot," she said. "Calvin was giving me a rub. What are you doing here?"

Heather took another step into the room and I noticed her feet were bare. "Me, too," she said. "Sore foot."

"I'll bet." Valerie's eyes swung to look at me. "You said you never matriculated."

"I don't," I blurted. "Tell her Heather."

Instead of answering, Heather looked from me to Valerie, and to my surprise, she laughed. "Why, Calvin, aren't you the little devil."

Valerie snickered. "He's not too good with backs, but he's great with feet."

"Wait a minute," I said. "I was just getting—"

I never got to finish my defense. Liza, wearing just the top of her pajamas, suddenly appeared in the doorway. "What's going on here?" she said in a voice that caused me to wish the police had dragged me away.

"Nothing, nothing," I said. "They had sore feet."

"Sore feet?"

"That's right," Valerie said. She stood up and went to the door. "Come on, Heather. I think she wants her feet rubbed."

"I do not," Liza snapped.

Heather grinned at her. "You should. I understand he's also good at matriculating."

She and Valerie were laughing as they walked away down the hall. But Liza wasn't laughing, or even smiling.

"I told you," she said, "what would happen if you started fooling around with the girls."

106

"I wasn't," I said. "I was in bed, sleeping, when Valerie came in. She had a sore foot. Then Heather came and...and...I'm innocent."

Liza started at my stricken face for what seemed like forever before she shook her head and said, "Well, don't let it happen again."

"I won't," I said. "Scouts honor. I'll keep my door locked no matter what."

"See that you do." She started to turn away, then suddenly turned back. "What was that about matriculating?"

I felt my face grow warm. "Oh, that. They misunderstood. They thought matriculating meant ...uh...something else...and...well, when I said I didn't, well...they misunderstood."

She suddenly put her hand over her mouth and quickly went out the door. The way she kept her hand over her mouth and the way her shoulders were shaking as she walked away made me wonder what I'd said that made her cry. But then, who understands women?

CHAPTER 11

As usual, it was Liza pounding on my door that rousted me out of bed before noon the next day.

Her first words after I managed to find my way to the door and she charged in waving a newspaper under my nose were, "We've got a problem."

I'd learned that when Liza said, 'We've got a problem' the day was not going to go well for me. My first thought was 'so what else is new?' My second thought was that she looked surprisingly lovely after being up so late. And my third thought was how could I escape?

I tried to maneuver around her, hoping I could get in bed and pull the covers over my head, but she took hold of my arm.

"We're late," she snarled. "A week.. They scheduled us here a week late."

"Late?" I said. "Late for what?"

"The Corrida Goyesca. Can you believe it?"

"Corrida Goyesca? What's that?" I asked, although I was certain I really didn't want to know.

I was right.

"The bullfight festival. They have it every year. It's on our schedule."

I relaxed, almost smiling. "That's nice." Missing a bullfight festival was not something I deeply regretted.

"Nice?!" She again waved the newspaper under my nose. "It was last week!"

I rubbed sleep from my eyes. "So? No bullfight. The bulls'll love it."

"So!! We've *got* to have a bullfight."

Got to? Uh oh. That did not sound good. Afraid—-deeply afraid---of what was coming, I ventured: "Next year we'll come earlier."

I made another move toward the bed, but again she grabbed my arm. "Not next year," she gritted. "Today. We've got to have a bullfight today."

Today? The shaft of fear that pierced my mind jarred me fully awake. The word 'today' coupled with 'we've got a problem,' plus the way she clutched my arm, would have awakened Rip Van Winkle.

Still, I refused to give up. "So I guess we missed the bullfights. Big deal," I said, knowing all the time that it really was going to be a 'big deal' and one that I would not like.

"We've got to have a bullfight," she said through clinched teeth. "It's in our contract."

There were those nasty words again: 'In our contract.' I gave up the idea of getting back to bed. "Don't they have bullfights without a festival?" I asked, knowing all the time that her answer would be nerve shattering.

It was. She said, "No. Not for another week."

I tried a nonchalant shrug, which is hard to do with someone clamping a death grip on your arm. "So we come back next week."

"We can't come back. In two days we're scheduled to be in Granada."

"They must have bullfights in Granada. This is Spain. They've got bullfights everywhere."

"I don't think so. Not Granada."

"Oh, Well, I guess we'll have to think of a substitute. Maybe I could do another flamenco..."

She shuddered as though someone had walked across her grave. "No. It's got to be a bullfight." I finished the words with her... "It's in the contract."

"Okay," She had let go of my arm, but by now I was wide awake so instead of diving into the bed I went to my window and pulled back the drapes. Brilliant sunlight bursting into the room caused me to reel back, covering my eyes with my palms. "Lordy, Lordy," I gasped. "An atomic bomb."

"It's a beautiful day." I could tell by Liza's voice that she was not pleased by my reaction. But when she spoke again, I wished the bright light *had* been caused by an atomic blast.

"You'll have to do it" she said.

Her words forced me to sink to the edge of the bed. I took my hands away from my eyes so I could stare at her. "Me? Do what?" But I knew! I knew!

"Be a bullfighter."

She was not laughing, not even smiling. I slowly shook my head. "A bullfighter? I don't know anything about bullfighting. I've never even seen a bullfighting. Except in the movies. There was that old black-and-white with Tyrone Power on TMC a couple of years ago." Remembering how the movie had ended, I really shook my head. "I couldn't do that. Those bulls are dangerous. They've got horns like swords—"

"You've got to," She moved to stand it front of me. "It's in your contract."

That lousy contract again. I sincerely wished I'd read the fine print. My voice was a mere squeak when I said, "But...but...Can't we hire a bullfighter?".

"Too expensive. We can get the bullring this afternoon for free. I've talked to Pepe. He knows where we can borrow a costume for you."

"Costume?"

"They call it a 'suit of lights.' You've got to look

like the real thing." I sat stunned as she turned away, tapping her lips with her finger. "The only problem is getting a bull or two."

"Two?" I knew that would be a waste of money. I'd be dead after the first one.

"I'll talk to Pepe," she said. "Get dressed. It's time for lunch. Don't mention it to the girls." She went to the door. "After lunch, pretend to be sick again. And when you get in the ring, try to make it look good. They're expecting a real bullfighter."

After she left, the thought that went through my mind was "But I'll bet they're not expecting the bull to win."

CHAPTER 12

Judging by the bullring's dressing room for bullfighters, this really was the oldest bullring in Spain. The room, situated somewhere beneath the stadium, was rather small and smelled musty as though some of the ancient bullfighters who had occupied the room had left their sweaty clothes behind. The only light come from small windows set high in the back wall, but even the dim light couldn't dim the brilliance of the heavily embroidered jacket and pants that Pepe had found for me.

"The suit-of-lights," he said. He held up the jacket. "*Muchas* sequins. In the old days, they used real jewels. The matador could not afford to let his suit get gored by the bull. Today..." He shrugged. "Sequins are cheap."

I checked to see if there were any holes in the suit from bull's horns, but the sequins seemed to be all in place. Like the flamenco suit I'd worn, everything was a little small, and I had a real struggle to pull up the ankle-length knickers.

Helping me, Pepe said, "It was the *mas grande* I could find."

"They'll have to cut it off my dead body with a knife," I said.

"Oh, fighting the bull is not difficult," He said. "The great Pedro Romero killed more than six thousand."

"Six thousand?" I gasped. "That's a lot of bulls."

"Of course, that was in seventeen-fifty or sixty. The bulls were smaller then. Today---" He kissed his fingers. "A *toro bravo* is bred to fight to the death. I

112

have seen a big Muro bull with ten banderilleras in him fight for more than an hour before he killed the matador." He crossed himself, and I found it a little disconcerting that he was looking at me at the time.

I already wore the required white shirt and red necktie I'd worn as a flamenco dancer, and Pepe helped me force my way into the sequined jacket.

I was pulling on the white knee-high socks when Pepe held up a pair of traditional slippers with black bows of ribbon. Looking at my feet he shook his head and put the slippers aside. "Like the flamenco," he said. "*Usa la zapatas* of your own."

Which seemed like good advice. At least I would die without my feet hurting.

Pepe helped disguise my brogans by pulling the bows off the traditional slippers and fastening them on my shoes with medical tape, of which he seemed to have a disconcerting supply.

When I finally stood up, the pants were so tight I could hardly walk, but after forcing my body through a few exercises the tight pants loosened a little. But I couldn't see myself springing out of the path of a charging bull with much alacrity.

"Here." Pepe handed me a black matador beret. "I think this once belonged to the great Manolete. It will bring you luck."

"Manolete." I positioned the beret on my head like the real matadors wore it: low in front and kind of flopping over my ears. "Didn't he retire a couple of years ago."

"In a way," he said, again crossing himself which I did not take to be a good sign. I was right because he added, "He was killed by a bad bull in 1947."

113

Suddenly the beret did not feel as though it carried a lot of good luck. I considered giving it back to him, but decided I might need it to throw at the bull as a distraction while I was running. Any sane bull would much rather gore something that belonged to the great Manolete than the skinny buttocks of some stupid American.

While positioning the beret on my head, I caught a glimpse of myself in a huge mirror, and caught my breath. I had to admit I looked good. I could hardly move, but in the suit-of-lights and with the beret and a fake mustache, I looked really, really cool.

"My *muleta*," I said to Pepe. "Where's my *muleta*?"

Pepe looked puzzled. "Como? You're what?"

"My cape? Every matador has a cape."

"Oh. *La muleta*." He unfolded a red cape and handed it to me. It was about four feet square, and I tried it with a couple of classic matador moves I'd seen Tyron Power do in the movie. It seemed like a pretty flimsy barrier to put between me and a charging, thousand pound bull.

"Do you have a bigger one?" I asked.

"Pepe shook his head. "No, *señor.*"

"How about the color? Doesn't red make the bull kind of crazy. Do you have one in white?"

"*Blanca*? No, *señor.*"

"How about purple? Royal purple." Pete's contemptuous stare would have withered cactus, but it was my life at stake. "Pink. Pink shouldn't make him too mad."

Pepe shook his head. "*Rojo solomente.*" He looked at his watch. "Ten minutos."

He started for the open doorway leading to the passage to the arena, "*Venga*," he said, jerking his head for me to follow him. "It is time."

"Wait," I remembered something from the old movie. "What about those guys on the horses? The ones who stick those spears in the bull to tire him out. Have they come in?"

"*El picadors?*" He shrugged. "We have little dinero. No *picadors*." He kept walking.

"Wait!" I cried. "My sword! Where is my killer sword?"

He did not slow down or even turn his head as he said, "No *espada*. You will not need *el espada*."

I wouldn't need the sword used to give the bull the *coupe de grâce?* What did he mean by that? It seemed to me it showed a certain lack of confidence in my ability to subdue the bull.

Before he reached the exit, Pepe had to change course to make room for Liza who was striding toward us.

"Ten minutes," she said to Pepe as they passed.

"*Si, señorita*," Pepe answered. "*Dies minutos. El toro* will be ready."

Liza came into the room, and I swept my hat off and made a sweeping bow. "We who are about to die, salute you," I said.

Actually, I wasn't as concerned about my coming demise as I could have been. In high school I had lettered in track, and while my specialty had been middle distance running, I was right up there with the champions in the dashes, hurdles, and long jump. Even without the picadors and *banderilleros* to slow him down I figured that a bull carrying a thousand or more pounds couldn't be too agile.

115

On the other hand, some of those deceased matadors must have been pretty fast on their feet. And I'd heard that those bulls were chosen for their speed and also were well trained. They had to know every trick of the trade. Maybe there was more to this bull fighting than I thought.

Even so, with the bull's lance-like horns as an added incentive, I was sure I could stay out of its reach long enough to tire it out. If worst came to worst, I could always leap out of the bull ring, although I would hate to appear a coward in front of the girls.

Oh, but wait a minute. They wouldn't know it was me. I was supposed to be back in the hotel, sick. They'd just think I was some cowardly Spanish matador.

"I need a name," I said. "Something like Manolete, Junior."

"I want to talk to you about that," Liza said.

A small shaft of hope broke through my black cloud of doubt. Maybe she was going to call off the spectacle. I tried to keep the eagerness out of my voice when I answered, "Talk? Yes. I agree. We've got to talk. Talk is good. Say for about an hour."

"I don't want you to get hurt," she said. "If things get dicey, run behind those barriers they have around the arena."

My idea exactly. Still, I had to be cool, so I said, "Run? In front of the girls? I'll look like a coward."

"But you'll be alive."

She had a point. "I used to be real good at track and field," I said. "I'll just stay out of his way 'til he gets tired and gives up. Pepe says I don't have to kill him."

"Well," she said. "Don't worry about it. We have

116

really good health insurance. Good all over the world."

If she thought that would make me feel better, she was wrong. I thought her advice about running behind one of those barriers was the best advice I'd heard so far. I just hoped my reluctance to look like a coward in front of a stadium full of people would not get me killed.

"How big a crowd do we have?" I asked.

"No crowd," she said. "This is a private show."

"Private? Only the girls?"

"That's right. They're all excited. They've never seen a bull fight."

That was good. They wouldn't be expecting too much. "How about you?" I asked. "Are you an aficionado?"

She shook her head. "I only saw one once. In that movie based on a Hemmingway book."

Oh, yeah. I didn't remember the book, but I knew Hemmingway had been a big fan of bullfighting.

Liza had been staring at me. Now she said, "You really look great in that outfit."

"Really?" I struck a poise as though I were about to dispatch a bull with a quick sword thrust. "I might take this costume home," I said.

"It's rented," she said. "Don't get blood on it."

As she walked out the door I stared after her, wondering whose blood she meant. I had the suspicious feeling she was not talking about the bull's.

I just had time for a couple of final poses in front of the mirror before it was time to make my entrance. I was concentrating so much on what sort of entrance I would make into the arena that I almost forgot my cape and had to run back and get it.

Just before I stepped out into the brilliant sunlit

117

arena, I paused to consider my entrance. I decided that running out waving the cape and taking bows would be too ostentatious. I settled on a shoulders back, strutting swagger, while lifting my hat in a friendly gesture to the crowd.

The 'crowd' proved to be the four girls and Liza sitting in the front row of the empty stadium. They did applaud with vigor augmented by a few shrill whistles, but their adulations sounded a little puny in the huge stadium.

I don't know how Pepe managed to arrange it, but when I reached the center of the arena, a blast of trumpets exploded from the arena's loudspeakers just as thick wooden gates at the far end of the area swung open and I saw the dreaded head and horns of *el toro*.

I braced myself, unfurling my red cape, preparing to leap about ten feet in the air when the bull charged.

And as though the red cape was an irresistible challenge, the two massive horns of the bull rushed toward me.

The two horns?! Where was the rest of the bull?

I stared. The loudspeakers died. The crowd's applause and whistling died in a ragged retreat.

The 'bull,' the deadly '*el toro*' consisted of a fake bull's head with two huge horns tied to the front of a two-wheeled cart that had handles so it could be pushed like a wheelbarrow. And pushing it as fast as his legs would take him, was Pepe!

The deadly-looking horns came at me in a swift charge with Pepe's feet kicking up dust and his teeth bared in a maniacal snarl that would have done credit to a real bull.

But I knew exactly what to do: holding my cape

118

shoulder high in a graceful *pechos*, I stomped my feet, shouting, "*Toro*. Come on *toro*!"

On he came, careening across the arena, the deadly horns aimed directly at my stomach. At the last second, just when it seemed I would surely be impaled, I yanked the cape back and stepped aside in a graceful pirouette. Naturally, the 'crowd' erupted with shouts, whistles and wild applause.

And for the next few minutes it was the duel of the ages as the 'bull' tried to impale me on its horns while, I, in graceful disdain, made pass after pass, each one closer than the last until the 'bull' collapsed to his knees, his head hanging in defeat while I strutted around him in an arrogant show of disdain that would have done credit to the great Manolete.

I was not surprised when the girls sprang from the stands and raced toward me across the sands of the arena. Magnanimously, I spread my arms, ready to accept their hugs and kisses of pure adulation.

"Me, Me," the lovely Dawn shouted and yanked the *muleta* from my outstretched hand.

"*En guarde*!" the beautiful Heather shouted as she yanked the handles of the 'bull' away from the defeated Pepe. Whipping the 'bull' around, she charged Dawn who waved her cape, then moved aside in a beautiful pass.

"Me, Me." Maria had no cape but she jumped, waved a handkerchief and shouted until Heather, with a roar, spun her 'bull' and charged her so that Maria had to leap aside to avoid the deadly horns.

And then the gorgeous Valerie leaped into the fray, taunting the 'bull' until it whipped around and charged and she sprang aside at the last second.

And it went like that for I don't know how many

119

minutes. The girls were all in good physical condition and it seemed they would never grow tired, twisting, turning, leaping, taunting the 'bull' into more and more dangerous passes. And when the 'bull' seemed to tire another girl grabbed the handles and did her best to impale the other girls and, sometimes, me. Was I wrong or did the 'bull' put a little more umph into its charge when directed at me?

I decided not to stick around and find out.

Pepe, also fearing for his life, crawled to the side of the arena where I had taken shelter and we both stood watching the berserk ladies.

Then, to my huge surprise, Liza ran into the arena. I assumed it was to stop the mele, but, no. She was in there stomping her feet in the dust, using her hat as a *muleta,* taunting the 'bull' into charging just like the others as she moved aside in a graceful pirouette.

The battle became so frantic and the 'bull's' charges so vicious they kicked up so much dust the action was difficult to follow, and I expected any second to hear a scream of anguish as the 'bull's' sharp horns found a succulent target.

I was doubly amazed when Liza's turn came to be the 'bull' and she laughed and shouted with joy as she chased the girls around the arena. What had happened to her cold reserve? She was having the time of her life, and watching her with her hair flying and eyes sparkling, I wondered if she'd ever before allowed herself to have so much fun.

It must have been minutes, but it seemed like an hour before the dust started to settle as, one by one, the exhausted girls collapsed on the sand.

I thought I should go out and make sure they

120

were all alive, but I was not about to get involved with that pack of valkyries until I was sure they were all too tired to move.

Still, it might be a good time to evaluate how each one had behaved during the "bullfight." I assumed that the pampered rich one would have reacted to a mock bullfight with less spirit than the others. After all, she probably was so world-weary that such antics would not even induce a smile of amusement.

No such luck. As I remembered the battle, they all had enjoyed it tremendously, throwing themselves into the skirmish time and again just as though it were a salsa dance and the bull was some macho male they had to render impotent.

When I finally girded up my courage enough to make the move, I went over to them and found that all five were not only unscathed, they were laughing.

"That was the best bullfight I ever saw," Heather said.

"Me to," Valerie agreed.

"Can we do it again, Liza?" Dawn said.

Liza stood up, brushing dust from her clothes. "I don't think so. We only got the arena for a couple of hours."

I hoped no one heard my sigh of relief. With my luck, they would probably find a real bull and guess who would be the human sacrifice. I looked up at the sun. "Let's get out of the sun," I said. "Too much sun is bad for the complexion."

"That's right," Dawn chimed in. "I burn like crazy."

Animated by the thought of sunburn, they scrambled to their feet and practically sprinted to the

121

shady area of the vast amphitheater.

As I followed with Liza she said, "Whose idea was that?"

I hesitated before answering. Did she consider using a fake bull a breach of contract? If so, was she looking for someone to blame? And guess who that would that be? But if she thought it was a brilliant strategy, I would be smart to take credit. Actually, I knew it was Pepe's idea. Obviously, he hadn't been able to acquire a real bull so he had come up with the substitute.

But thus far he had said nothing, so I could probably bring it off if I took credit.

On the other hand, if Liza felt it was a really bad idea, it would be smart to allow Pape to take credit.

So what should I do?

I solved the problem by avoiding it. Instead of heading for the place where the girls were now sitting in a shady part of the bull ring, I changed direction toward the exit to the dressing room. "Tell you later," I said. "Right now I've got to get out of this suit. It's killing me. Way too small."

"Okay," she said, taking the bait. "But be careful when you do. It's a rental."

"Right. Careful it is."

I almost sprinted for the exit only taking time to make a couple of passes with my *muleta* to remind Liza and the girls that I could have put on a great show if I'd had to fight a real bull. They might even have given me one of the bull's ears as a reward. On the other hand, if the bull had won, would they have awarded it one of my ears? More likely both.

CHAPTER 13

We would not be leaving for Granada until tomorrow so that allowed us to launch into the girls' favorite part of the tour: seeing how long they could go without sleep.

Ronda, like every city in Spain seemed to come alive after the sun went down. Being a relatively small city, however, it did not have the vast numbers of bars found in the big cities. The few it did have made up for their small numbers with great varieties of *tapas*, including grilled shrimp, stuffed crab, cured ham, and clams simmered in garlic and parsley.

Every bar, it seemed, had a band that featured the requisite accordion and two or more guitar players. Even though the musicians looked bored as though they had been playing the same songs over and over for about a hundred years, they managed to whip out spirited music for some Spanish dances that I'd learned were called *coplas.*

Although dancing the *coplas* sounded exciting, after my adventures in the bull ring I didn't feel much like flinging myself around a minuscule dance floor. When the girls tried to entice me into dancing, I first used my excuse for, supposedly, missing the bullfight because, as they had been led to believe, I'd been sick.

They kind of grimaced as though they didn't believe me, and it led me to wonder why they hadn't seen through my disguise as a bullfighter. We'd been practically nose to nose in the bull ring, but they had given no indication that they were being hoodwinked. It had to be because they were having too much fun concentrating on the 'bull.' Well, as they say, 'whatever

123

works.'

Now, instead of pretending to be sick, I found a better means to avoid dancing: spending all my time at the tapas bar. I never cared much for clams, but by holding my nose I was able to slurp down about five of the gooey, garlic-spiced clams. After ingesting all that garlic, all I had to do was breath hard and it was not only the girls who shunned me; even Liza kept her distance.

Actually, I think the fevered Spanish atmosphere was having its affect on Liza because she kicked up such a storm on the dance floor that even the girls paused in their gyrations to stare at her. Not much finesse but a lot of energy and even some unbelievable hip twitching. The Spanish men, of course, all loved it. Even though there seemed to be a plethora of lovely Spanish girls---or I assumed they were Spanish---with long legs, slender bodies and masses of long, dark hair---the young men, all of whom looked like scraggly-haired college sophomores, seemed to prefer the American girls.

By making periodic trips to savor the garlicky clams at the *tapas* bar and staring in amazement at the incredibly energetic dancers, I was able to stay awake. However, by 2:00 o'clock in the morning I either had to abandon my responsibilities and head back to the hotel, or find some way to make my body believe I was having a great time.

One method I found to keep myself semi-alert was to think about the two paparazzi goons. I hadn't seen them since we left Seville, and I wondered if we had managed to lose them. My trepidations caused me to get up every once in a while and saunter around the room, checking the nooks and even the rest rooms for

124

signs of the two. A couple of times I even went outside looking for the yellow car. But the cobble stoned street, too narrow for parked cars, was deserted. Even a big moon had trouble getting its beams between the ancient two and three story apartment buildings that hugged the narrow sidewalks.

I didn't waste much time looking. At two o'clock in the morning an eerie fog of silence had settled over the street. The faint sound of music from the club only seemed to **add to the haunting** hush. Enveloped by the stillness, remembering every horror film I had ever seen, my body dredged up an involuntary shiver of dread. I was glad to go back inside the lively club.

Maybe it was just me and my droopy eyelids, but each dance seemed to go on forever. If I hadn't been charged up with worry about those two goons I really would have thrown in the towel. Or maybe it was the thought of walking back to the hotel alone in those eerie streets. Either way, I was sort of happy when, in the middle of a song, Maria left the dance floor and flounced toward me. I knew she was again going to ask me to dance. It had been some time since I recharged my breath with garlic, so I sort of slumped down in my chair trying to look sick and hoping that my garlicky breath still had the strength of an antisocial skunk.

But, surprise. She didn't ask me to dance. She flopped in a chair beside me and used one hand to fan her face. I hoped she was trying to fan away my breath. More likely she was attempting to fan away a few notes of the perpetual *copla* music before it drove her crazy.

She picked up her half-empty wine glass but only took a sip as though she didn't want the wine to dull her dance hormones. I kind of smiled at her to let her know I was still awake, but I didn't want to encourage her by talking so I kept my mouth shut.

"How you feeling?" she said. "You look awful."

I did? Oh, yeah. I assumed she was referring to my fake illness. But maybe not. She'd been dancing with those macho Spanish guys all evening. Compared to them I guess I did look a little anemic. My facial stubble was too light-colored and scraggly to give me that sexy scruffy look the girls all seemed to like, so I usually kept myself smooth shaven. A few tattoos would have helped my macho image, but if I had even my mother's name tattooed on my arm my folks would have killed me. I was, however, smart enough to know that any hint of a smile would destroy today's requisite bad-boy image. Who ever heard of a macho movie star who smiled? A sneer once in a while, yes. But a smile? Never. So I kept my lips pressed in a grim frown. But even then I knew my projected image was a far cry from motorcycle gang brute. I would just have to depend on my personality to give me the requisite devil-may-care machismo.

At the moment, however, surviving was more important than image, and surviving depended on keeping away from the dance floor.

"Better," I sort of croaked. "A little better." I punctuated the pronouncement with a couple of sickly coughs.

"Well, we'll be here a few days I guess. That'll give you time to get well."

"Oh, no," I said. "We'll be leaving in the morning. Not early morning. You know. The usual, after brunch."

"Really? Where?"

Where? I'd forgotten. Pamplona? No, that came later. Stalling for time, I searched my memory for

126

something. "A big city. Very modern. Lots of *tapas*. And a...ah...castle." That was good. Every Spanish. "It's called a...a." A name popped into my head. "Alambra. You'll love it."

"Alambra? Are you sure?"

The load of doubt dripping from her voice made me sure I would have gotten it wrong if she had asked me my name. "I think so," I said. "It's over by Madrid."

"Oh, I like Madrid. Lots of dance clubs. Can we stay there a few days?"

I'd forgotten about the Madrid night life. Well, I guess this is what they paid for. But a few days? That could be dangerous. By keeping on the move, it didn't give the macho guys a chance to prove their machismo was not simply an image of enchantment. It was best to keep moving, so I said, "The point is, we have to be in...uh...where we're going by tomorrow."

"Oh." She took another sip of her wine. "Do you know where we'll be staying? What hotel?"

I shook my head. "No. You'll have to ask Liza. That's her department."

"Oh, okay. I just thought I'd let my folks know."

Her folks? What did I know about Maria? Nothing. This might be the time to get some information.

"Your folks," I said. "Where do they live?"

She stared at me for a moment as her mind tried to grapple with my abrupt conversational about face. "My folks? San Fernando Valley. Why?"

Why, indeed? She'd said San Fernando Valley. That was in California? The other girls were, I believe, all from Arizona or Oklahoma or...wherever. I tried to remember the little background I had on Maria. "Oh, yes," I said as though I knew. "Your dad's in the trucking business. Or is it railroads?"

"Neither one. Markets. You've heard of Latino Markets."

"Well, no. Are they like Ralph's or Safeway?"

"Something like that. Mostly in the Valley and East L.A."

That didn't sound much like a multibillion dollar enterprise. Unless, of course, she was lying. I seemed to remember that all the girls were supposed to be in college somewhere so I said, "Right. I remember. You go to USC."

"UCLA. I'll be a senior this fall."

That was a clue. USC, the University of Southern California was privately owned. Very expensive. UCLA, on the other hand, was part of the state-operated University of California system. Not as likely that the richest girl in the world would matriculate there. Unless, of course, she were hiding her wealth by appearing to be just one of the poor proletariats like me.

"You into cars?" I asked. Everybody in California was into cars. The brand she drove would give me a clue.

"Not really. I have a Prius. You know. Save on gas."

Another clever ploy? A mega-rich girl driving a Prius? Who would suspect? "You going to take over the business, the family business, when you graduate? You know: off-shore bank accounts? Hedge funds? They teach you all that at UCLA?"

"No. I'm more into art."

Art? Could a billionaires be an artist? I suppose so. She wouldn't have to waste money on all those Van

128

Goghs or Picassos if she could paint them herself.

She shot that idea down when she said, "Computer art."

"You mean artistic art, like painting pictures? Or art like theater or motion pictures?"

"No. I'm into computer graphics. Animation."

"Oh, sure. Like Pixar. Dreamworks. Start your own company."

"I should be so lucky." She sort of cocked her head. "How about you? Heather said you're in college. The travel agency is just a summer job."

"That's right. University of Nevada. I've got two more years."

"Why Nevada? You're from Utah or somewhere like that."

"Idaho. Well, I..." Should I tell her I transferred from Idaho State to the University of Nevada because of a girl? That might be counterproductive. "Money really. It's a little cheaper in Nevada. I had invitations from Harvard, Stanford, MIT, but..." I gave her one of my best grins, designed to disguise the real reason for my next question. "Do you know where I can borrow about a million dollars?"

"No. But if you find out, let me know. I could use a few million."

Was she lying; just putting on an act?

I never got the chance to probe her brain any deeper. Surprisingly, the musicians were taking a break and Liza came to the table. I could see a fine sheen of perspiration on her face. The first thing she did was pick up her half-empty glass of Mouzo beer and drain it.

I silently prayed she wouldn't order another glass. That would mean at least another half-hour here, and I seriously doubted I could remain upright for more than a couple of minutes.

To my relief, she glanced at her watch and said, "We'd better get back to the hotel. We've got a long drive tomorrow. Go get the other girls."

The other girls were still on the dance floor talking to guys who looked as though they would not take kindly to someone upsetting their post-dance plans. So, I said to Liza, "You'd better come with me." I looked at Maria. "Right, Maria?"

She glanced toward the girls. "Yeah. Those guys might have other plans."

Looking at the guys, it didn't take an Einstein to guess what was going through their minds. I got up and waited for Liza to join me. "Stay close to me," I said.

We walked over to where the three girls were standing with the guys. During the short walk I managed to maneuver to a comfortable step or two behind Liza.

When we closed in on the girls and their hopeful gigolos, I was surprised to hear the guys speaking English, although their accents could use a little work. The girls, however, must have thought they sounded cute because they were giggling and laughing.

I don't know how she did it, but when we got close to the group, Liza was behind me. With little or no choice, I twisted my face into a forbidding grimace and got their attention by saying, "Well, ladies." I tapped my wristwatch. "Long day tomorrow. Time to go."

Heather thrust out her lovely lower lip. "Oh, not yet."

"It's not that late. One more dance," Dawn said.

130

The guy with Valerie put his arm around her waist possessively, saying, "*Venga*. The night is...how you say...young."

Fortunately, Liza stepped forward. "No. Come ladies. We have to go."

The girls looked at one another but it was Mr. Macho with Valerie who let go of her and bared his teeth at me in a grimace that was not a smile. "The ladies do not wish to go." He turned to Valerie. "Is *correcto*?"

Valerie hesitated before she said, "*Si. Correcto.*" She snapped her fingers. "*Muchas* dances."

"Wait a minute," I said---

That was as far as I got before the guy poked me in the chest with a finger. "How you say...get lost."

The guy had a scruffy beard, scraggly hair and hard dark eyes under thick eyebrows that made him look really tough. But I noticed his arms and legs in his tight shirt and pants looked kind of skinny as though he didn't spend a lot of time doing hard work. On the other hand, I'd grown up working on farms and, say what you want about modern farms with all their computers and machines, they still involved a lot of physical labor, and that developed muscle. So, while I might look skinny, I figured I was in a lot better shape that this dude.

So I grabbed the hand with the finger he'd poked in my chest and squeezed, as I said, "How you say in Spanish, get lost yourself, *stupido*?"

His eyes widened and he tried to pull his hand away, but I just squeezed harder. His chin lifted, his teeth gritted and his eyes squinted. The other two guys backed up a couple of steps. "*Comprende*?" I added with a beatific smile.

131

"*Comprendo*," the guy managed to say.

I let go of his hand and turned my smile on the three ladies, "Come on, ladies. Bedtime."

The girls looked toward the three guys, but they were already moving away, with one of them massaging his hand.

"Well," Dawn said. "You sure know how to ruin an evening."

But Heather was giving me a strange look. "Why, Calvin," she said. "**Where did that come from?**"

Even Liza's eyes had widened and her mouth was kind of open. She snapped her mouth shut, then turned to the girls. "Come. I think we'd better leave."

The sooner the better. I didn't want to give the guys time to round up reinforcements.

I was, however, a little surprised at how docile the girls were as they quickly gathered their things and walked out into the street. Maybe what I'd thought was going to be way over on the negative might turn out to be positive. Besides, I was wide awake when we walked out.

I guess it was the kind of eerie silence of the street after being pummeled by the music for a couple of hours, but none of the ladies said a word as we walked to the hotel, our steps echoing in the dark. I was more than a little surprised when Heather and Dawn took hold of my arms and we walked with their hips touching mine. Their desire to be so clingy was probably due to the spooky street, but it did feel pretty darn good. At least it did until I noticed Liza's frown, but I just pulled the girls in a little closer. I guess, like a fool, I was beginning to like living dangerously.

CHAPTER 14

Before we left the next day I called Mr. Kimberly in Phoenix to bring him up to date. Naturally, I said everything was hunky-dory. I didn't tell him about the make-believe bull fight. It might have cast a bad reflection on Liza because, after all, scheduling events was part of her duties. If her plans went awry, that couldn't be blamed on me, could it? However, on the assumption that anything that did not go according to plan would be laid at my door, I thought it would be prudent to give a good report.

But there was only one report that interested him. Right off the bat he asked, "Anything new on...uh...our subject?"

I didn't like to admit it but I was kind of forced to say, "Uh...no, sir. Nothing new."

There was a poignant little pause before he said, "And you're next stop is...," letting his voice trail off.

But I was ready. I'd looked up our itinerary and located our next stop on a map: a place called Grenada. It wasn't far from Rhonda. "Grenada," I said. "You know. Like in the song."

I hummed a few notes to let him know I was on top of it.

"Oh, right," he said. "Granada. I've been there. The Alhambra."

It occurred to me that since he'd been there he might be able to help me out with a few tips about the place that would make me look good. On the other hand he had probably picked me to be the tour guide because of my intelligence---which included being a quick study of tour guide books---so I used a subtle

133

approach. First I asked him, "Uh, Mr. Kimberly, what's an Alhambra?"

"The Alhambra?" He sounded a little startled. "That's a famous old Moorish citadel in Granada."

"Right. Old Moorish Alhambra. Also an Alcazar. Very old. You could say ancient."

I hope he picked up on my use of the word 'Alcazar,' whatever that was.

"Where are you now?"

"Rhonda," I said. "We're just leaving. In fact, I'd better cut this short. Wouldn't want to be left behind."

"I understand. Keep in touch."

He hung up. I was a little disappointed that I hadn't learned any little trade secrets from him that would have made me look erudite in front of the girls, but the drive to Granada would take three or four hours. Plenty of time to study my tour guides.

Actually, I didn't try too hard. The first half of the journey heading east out of Rhonda wound through the northern foothills of the Sierra Nevada range where views of the canyons and mountains were too spectacular to ignore. At least for me. As usual the girls proved once again that they could doze through a trip to the moon. Even Liza had given up trying to interject excitement into the long car rides and, despite the sway of the curves, she also tried to catch up on her sleep.

About halfway through the trip we picked up the main highway at a town called Antequera, and on a straight, smooth highway the ladies were able to get in some real sleep. I didn't know which view kept me awake: the views of the spectacular Sierra Nevada range outside or views of the five gorgeous ladies

134

lounging inside the SUV.

Despite the remarkable scenery, I, too, had started to doze off when we entered the outskirts of Grenada. It was what I'd managed to read about the history of the city during the short time I'd actually concentrated on my studies that jarred me awake. I wanted to see this city. I'd read that it was the last place in Spain that had remained under Moorish rule until it was conquered by the Spanish in 1492, long after the remainder of Spain had been conquered. The date was easy for me to remember because that was the same date King Ferdinand of Aragon and his queen Isabella of Castile made it possible for Columbus to discover the New World that today is called America. I figured that when I explained that to the girls, I would really sound profound.

The city of Granada is set at the base of a range of hills so that for miles before we reached the city I could see a massive structure sprawling across a hill so that it seemed to dominate the city. With the afternoon sunlight highlighting vast reddish-brick walls and battlements it was like a massive anvil that would crush any miscreant below. It had to be the fabled Alhambra, the huge fortress built by the Moors when they ruled southern Spain.

As we entered the city, evidence of the almost 800 years of Moorish domination was evident, with arabesque arches and filigreed facades in many of the buildings lining the streets. Typically for ancient cities, the side streets were a zigzag labyrinth. Cruising down the wide Gran Via de Colon---the only street I could see that was more than a block or two long---even allowed a passing glance of a nearby huge cathedral. When I pointed it out to the girls, who were beginning

135

to come awake, all they did was yawn. So much for ancient cathedrals.

Moving deeper into the city, I noticed there were colorful decorations on the fronts of buildings and on lamp posts. We were also forced to slow down by what I assumed to be an unusual number of people on the narrow sidewalks and jaywalking in the streets. Many of the people in the more crowed streets were decked out in festive costumes and garish masks.

"A festival," Pepe told me over his shoulder. "In Spain there's always a festival."

"Good," I said. "That means there won't be so many people at the Alhambra." |

He laughed. "Don't count on it. The Alhambra is very popular."

Just my luck.

"What festival is it?" Liza asked.

Pepe shook his head. "*No se.* Many places in Spain have their own festivals."

How Pepe was able to find his way to our hotel through the traffic and the maze of streets was a mystery.

I had just climbed out of the SUV in front of the hotel's neo-Moorish façade when between buildings I caught a glimpse of a scene that made me catch my breath.

Pepe saw me staring and said, "The Alhambra. Beautiful, no?"

From this point of view at the foot of the hill, the Alhambra was definitely imposing. My studies had told me the word 'Alhambra' meant the color 'red.' It was easy to see why. In the evening sunlight, the Alhambra was a massive reddish-colored brick fortress sprawling over an entire plateau on top of the hill, dominating

136

everything below.

I remembered that like so many castles, it had first been constructed as a fortress by some Moorish king in about 1238. But, unlike Pepe, the word that came to my mind was not 'beautiful'; it was 'forbidding.' I could only imagine what it must have been like to live in the city below, knowing that at any moment you could be crushed by a single word from the Lord of the Alhambra.

Judging by the size of the thing, it was going to require a lot of time to see even a fraction of the famous monument.

Then I remembered that my tour group did not tend to linger over either architecture or objects of art, and we could probably do the whole Alhamba in about an hour, unless, of course, there were also some fashionable shops scattered around the facility.

Moving into the hotel took more than an hour even with a couple of bellman practically breaking their backs unloading the SUV and trucking the ladies' baggage to their rooms. But once we were settled in, we all met in the hotel restaurant for a late lunch, at least I called it "lunch." At home I would have called it an early supper.

As usual, the girls all sported totally different wardrobes, including shoes, and I wondered if they had some kind of unspoken competition going to see which one would the first to wear the same clothes twice. Judging by their number of bags and the way they loved shopping, I didn't think any of them would lose.

Liza, apparently, was not in the running because, while she dressed almost as well as the girls, she occasionally mixed up some previously-worn pieces with new ones.

137

With the area being situated in the Sierra Nevada Range's foothills, the weather, unlike at Granada, was relatively cool, allowing the ladies to don clothes that looked as though they had been designed for fall, with cute caps and hats and long pants and sweaters, which was fine with me. I loved sweaters.

I also thought that observing the clothes the girls wore would give me a few clues about who might be the wealthy one. You know: Real diamond bracelets, thousand-dollar pointy-toed shoes, drop-dead red lipstick. Stuff like that. No way. It didn't work. I don't know how they did it, unless all their parents were pretty well off, but it didn't look to me as though any of their clothes came off the discount racks. I also discovered that, these days it's impossible for an amateur like me to tell authentic Tom Ford shoes or a genuine Oscar De La Renta bag from made-in-China knockoffs.

That reminded me: it had been so long since I'd seen any evidence of our paparazzi stalkers I'd almost forgotten my secondary job of watching out for the girls' welfare. But I also figured that unless those goons were psychic, they would have had a tough time tracking us through the city's maze of streets.

Even so, after our supper/lunch, when we went through the hotel's lobby toward the entrance, I made it a point to check out everyone in sight. I was not only trying to spot either of the paparazzi goons, but anyone else who looked suspicious. I reasoned that by this time, if somehow the paparazzi goons had gotten wind that one of the girls was the daughter of one of the richest men in the world, other people with nefarious schemes might also have found out.

But everything looked copasetic, which led me

138

to wonder: would I recognize a crook or a paparazzo if I saw one? With my vast lack of experience, probably not. Still, it wouldn't hurt to be alert.

I didn't think any of us was looking forward to trudging up the hill to the Alhambra, but, thankfully, Pepe drove us up to the old fortress' entrance.

After Liza took care of our tickets, we passed through the massive outer wall through a quintessential Moorish horseshoe-shaped passageway, and immediately found ourselves in a large open area surrounded by what appeared to be the remains of buildings. Liza turned to me, nodded toward the girls, and kind of whispered, "Okay. They're all yours."

My heart leaped. Four lovely girls, all mine!

Reality hit me so quickly I was amazed. She meant 'they were all mine' as their tour guide. Well, I was ready.

"This area," I told them, "is called the 'Alcazaba,' which means...uh...fortress."

The girls stared at an array of low stone walls that could have been foundations for former structures.

"What happened to the buildings?" Valerie asked.

"Napoleon," I immediately answered. "When he conquered Spain, he tried to destroy this whole complex. But he only destroyed this Alcazaba part when he got defeated and had to quit."

"Why did he want to tear it down?" Maria said.

"Why?" I had no idea, so I said, "It was a fortress. He destroyed every fortress he found."

Dawn had been looking at the surrounding barren walls, "Boooreing," she said.

"This isn't the good part," I told her. "Follow me."

139

I led them to the far end of the area where five large arches opened in a massive wall. On the other side we found a huge garden area fragrant with the scent of profuse rose bushes. Looking around, what immediately struck me was the contrast between the massive outside walls and turrets of the ancient fortress and the delicate work within the thick walls. Everywhere I looked: the facades, the archways, the slender columns supporting filigreed ceilings, looked **as though they had** been meticulously **wrought** by loving artists. I was fascinated by the geometric structures, the delicate carvings of leaves, flowers, arabesques, and stalactite-fringed arches.

"This is the high garden," I volunteered with crossed fingers. "It was called '*the Generalife*'."

The girls weren't so impressed. Looking at the vast garden, Valerie gave an expressive, "Boooreing."

"This is nothing," I said leading the way. "Wait 'til we get inside the palace area."

We practically ran through the palace's 'bath section' into and area with a long, shallow pool of water. The pool was narrow, but about the length of an Olympic pool. At one end was a huge building with a tower.

"This is called the Court of the Myrtles," I told the girls. "That building at the end leads to a famous room where Columbus talked the King into giving him the money to make his voyage to America."

I started walking on the cement border of the pool toward the building. Liza and three of the girls started to follow me, but Heather pointed to an arched doorway on our right.

"What's in there?"

I stopped, searching my recalcitrant memory,

"The royal palace. Nothing much there except the living quarters, a couple of gardens and the harem quarters."

"Harem," she said. "I want to see that."

"Me, too," Dawn said.

Before I could distract them with my beautifully prepared dissertation about the filigreed walls and ceiling of the famous *Salon de Embajadores*, they were heading for the entrance to the inner palace.

Liza and I hurried to catch up. The ladies had stopped just beyond the entrance in the rose covered garden area and were staring at an alabaster fountain surrounded by twelve rather crudely carved images of lions.

"Where is the harem?" Heather said.

I wasn't about to bypass all my book learning so I said, "We'll get to that. This courtyard is called the Patio of the Lions. One of the most famous areas in all of Spain. It was built by the Moors. As you can see there are twelve lions, one for each month. Originally, water came out of the mouth of the lion-of-the-month. And there's a story---"

Valerie interrupted me. "Where is the harem?"

I looked at Liza for support, but she just made a small shrug.

I gave up trying to sound intelligent. "This way," I muttered.

I led them through another horseshoe-shaped doorway that opened to a large salon with a beautifully filigreed ceiling that I would liked to have examined, but which I knew would be of little interest to the girls. I did, however, point out two large slabs of cement on the floor. "These are the graves of twin girls."

Without pausing I led them into the next room.

141

It was a long, narrow room with a beautifully filigreed ceiling but without a stick of furniture. I hoped the girls wouldn't ask me the purpose of the room because I had no idea.

Walking the few steps across the room to one of several window-like openings on the far side our steps echoed eerily off the bare walls, and I remembered reading that this room was famous for its strange acoustics in that a whisper in one end of the long room could easily be heard at the other end, sort of like the rotunda of St. Peters basilica in London where a whisper at one side of the rotunda could be heard on the far side.

But my desire to give the peculiar acoustics a try would have to wait. The girls were already at the windows that provided an excellent view of a large garden strewn with the ubiquitous roses.

"Where's the harem?" Maria said. "I don't see any harem."

"Me neither," Heather added. "You said this was the harem."

"This is it," I said. "It's called the Padio of the Harem." I pointed to a small ornate building on the far side of the garden. "That small building was the sultan's boudoir where he'd take members of his harem for a...a nap or...uh...whatever."

"How many girls in his harem?" Dawn asked.

"How many did he take with him to his boudoir?" Valerie said.

"Probably one," Heather said. "That's all one man can handle. Right, Calvin?"

How would I know? I was about to make up a satisfactory number like six or seven, but Liza beat me to the punch.

142

"He was only allowed four wives," she said.

"But how many harem girls?" Maria said.

"About a hundred I bet," Dawn chimed in.

Valerie snickered, "I'll bet one could have killed him."

"I pity those poor wives," Marie said. "They wouldn't get any action at all."

"Not true," Liza said. "They had to produce heirs to the throne. The sultan had to...uh...keep them happy until he got a son. Hopefully, more than one."

"Yeah," I said. "He needed more than one. In those days for a son to live long enough to take over the kingdom was pretty problematical

"With all those harem girls and four wives, how did he find time to run a kingdom?" Valare said.

"Didn't have to, really," Liza answered. "He had a wizer and a whole staff of people to do that for him."

Heather shook her head. "I bet some of them helped him out with the harem, too."

"If they did," I said, "and he found out, their heads would roll."

"Right," Maria said. "That's why all the men servants were eunuchs."

"That must have been awful," Dawn said. "All those women and you couldn't do a thing with them."

Valerie laughed. "I'll bet the women weren't too thrilled either."

Dawn moved to the doorway, "Well, I've seen enough castles. Let's go find a place where the men like to dance."

Following her out the door, Heather and Marie quickly agreed.

As she passed me Valare nudged me with her elbow, "How about you, Calvin? Would you rather have been a sultan or a eunuch?"

Before I could answer Liza gave me a sidelong look. "You'd better not get any Sultan ideas or you will be a eunuch."

As the ladies walked out, I lingered a moment, staring down at the garden, trying to picture myself as a sultan, knowing there were about a hundred sex-starved women waiting for me. It was the kind of dream most men wished for. On the other hand, a man had to know his limits. But what a glorious way to die.

I turned and followed the girls. They were just going out the door on the other side of the hall when two men wearing festival costumes brushed by them entering the long hall. The girls, all of them talking at once, paid no attention to the men. At first neither did I. After all, hundreds of people visited the famous structure every day. Thus far we had been lucky because most of the people who would be touring the Alhambra were in the city participating in the festival. Many of those who did make the visit still wore their fiesta costumes, some with comical masks like these two, so at first I paid little attention to them.

Then something made me turn to watch them. They were hurrying toward the far end of the hall, and I wondered why. There was nothing there, not even a window or door.

Still, it was none of my business and I started to turn to leave when a tingle of alarm made me stop just outside the exit. I peered around the edge of the doorway to watch the two. They were about the same height, but one was slender and the other heavy, burly. The two paparazzi goons! Simon and Bruno. I was sure of it.

I was about to step back into the hall to confront

them when I heard a harsh whispered voice say, "Damn." The voice was so close I jerked my head around, looking for someone beside me. There was no one.

The voice said, "We're running out of time. We've got to make it today."

I knew that voice, even if it was a whisper: Simon, the skinny goon.

My lord. It was true. The empty hall really was a perfect acoustical chamber. I was hearing the men at the far end of the hall.

Now Bruno said, "We could grab her here."

Simon snorted. "We don't know which one, you moron. We can't take them all."

"Sure we can. They came in that SUV. When they get in to go back, we take it with them inside."

There was a pause as though Simon was too surprised by Bruno's scheme to answer. Finally he said, "Naaa. We'd never get out of town. We've got to get her alone."

"But we don't know which one."

"Don't matter. Neither do they. We just grab one, tell 'em it's the right one, and bada-bing, bada-bang, we're finished."

Bruno's laugh was so loud it almost broke my eardrum. "Yeah," he said. "Bada-bing, bada-bang."

I figured the acoustic anomaly would work both ways so I lowered my voice into a deep growl, stuck my mouth close to the wall and said, "You touch even one of those broads and I'll lock you up in a Spanish dungeon."

They both jerked their heads back and forth looking for the source of the voice, but I had ducked back out of sight.

145

I walked away, hurrying to catch up with the girls. I was pretty sure they would be safe now, at least while those goons believed the place was haunted.

But I was also haunted, haunted by the question: how did they know where we would be?

CHAPTER 15

It's a long drive from Granada to Madrid, so the next morning Liza somehow got us up and having breakfast by ten o'clock. Liza took care of the hotel bill while I sat at a table with the girls trying to remember where we were.

After dancing away half the night, the girls were almost as groggy as I was, but when Liza rejoined us-—looking so buoyant I almost hated her--Maria surprised me by asking, "Where are we going next, Liza?"

What surprised me about her question was that she should know our next destination. I was pretty sure the girls had all been given our itinerary. But I guess they hadn't bothered to read it, or they expected our little adventure to be full of pleasant surprises where we were going.

"I hope it's somewhere with guys who know how to dance," Dawn added with a yawn.

Since that could be anywhere in Spain, and since Liza was occupied studying a map, I answered for her, "Pomplona." I glanced at my watch. "It'll be a long ride. Almost five hundred miles."

"Five hundred miles? In one day?"

"Oh, no. I believe we stop in Madrid tonight, then finish the trip tomorrow. Right, Liza?"

Liza looked up from the map. "That's right. Madrid first. It's on the way."

"Oh, I like Madrid," Valerie said. "Lots of shops and dance places. Can we stay there a few days?"

I winced. I wasn't sure I could live through more than one night of Madrid's night life. But I guess this is what they paid for. Even so--a few days? I shuttered. "Liza," I said, "Didn't you say we had to be in Pamplona in time for something about bulls."

"Madrid first," Liza said. "One night. Then Pamplona for the running of the bulls."

One night? If I slept through most of the long drive, I would survive one night. Couldn't I?

"Oh" Maria said. "Running of the bulls. I've heard of that."

"Me, too." Valarie chimed in. "That's where bulls chase people, isn't it?"

Liza nodded. "That's right. Very exciting."

Dawn let out a squeal. "Can we do it? Can we get in the chase?"

"No, no," Liza quickly squashed the idea. "It's far too dangerous. People are always getting gored. Some even killed."

"Oh, poo," Marie pouted. "Just watching is no fun."

"It will be," Liza said. "You'll love it. Won't they, Calvin?"

"Oh, sure," I agreed. "Big festival. Lots of excitement."

Heather said. "I'm mixed up. I thought our next stop was someplace with nude beaches."

Nude beaches? I suddenly didn't feel sleepy anymore. The though of the four girls on a nude beach was definitely a wakerupper. But there were no beaches in Pamplona "Uh, are you sure?" I said.

Liza ruined my euphoria by emphatically saying, "No. It's Pamplona. No beaches." She folded the map as she jerked her head at the girls. "Come," she said. "It's a long way to Madrid. Let's get started."

She got up and walked away and the four girls

148

dutifully followed, talking to each other excitedly, leaving me disappointed that I hadn't found even one clue about which one was the worldly-wise billionaires.

However, what Heather had said about nude beaches swirled through my mind. driving away all other thoughts, as I followed the ladies. I didn't remember *that* being on my list. I sure hoped my list was wrong. Wow. I could hardly wait.

But first things first.

I tried to force my concupiscent mind into safer channels: Think of Pamplona. What did I know about one of the oldest cities in Spain? Nothing except it's the home of something called The Running Of The Bulls. But Liza would have planned something more entertaining than watching a herd of bulls chasing people, an event that would be over in minutes. Then what? Cathedrals? Castles? Thank heavens practically every Spanish city had a castle. I had to find a few guide books, hopefully, ones with a lot of pictures. Of course, there was always shopping.

But for now I had to find a way to survive an evening of making the rounds of Madrid's *tapas* bars. Ruminating about nude beaches would surely help.

An hour later we were heading north. As usual, the girls were all asleep before we'd even left the outskirts of the ancient city. Or what passed for sleep because the way the highway twisted and turned through the southern Andelusian mountains kept them swaying first one way then back the other.

Clinging to my seat behind them, surrounded by shifting luggage, my eyes wanted to sleep but my continuously buffeted body would not allow it. Then too, my mind was buffeted by the mystery of the four girls. Which was the golden girl? We had been together

149

for several days now, and I had made absolutely no progress toward solving the puzzle. The only one I hadn't been able to engage in a one-on-one conversation was Heather, but it was hard to believe that such a vivacious beauty had been able to endure isolation all her life. Even pampered isolation. Still, I would have to find some way to have a little time alone with her. The problem was not only to separate her from the other girls, but to separate her from Liza. As the days flew by and she saw the way the girls were becoming more friendly toward me, the more her suspicious instincts were heightened.

As usual she was sitting up front in the passenger seat beside Pepe. I could see the back of her head as she sat bolt upright, her back straight, staring straight ahead. When we swept around a curve, the girls swayed like willows in a breeze, but she hardly swayed at all. If she were sleeping or even dozing, she had to have an iron subconscious to hold the ridged pose. But with her will power, it was probably easy.

The way I was being flung about my own willpower had to be far weaker than hers, or smarter, which might be a good thing because, except for brief interruptive thoughts of Spanish nude beaches, my sleep-deprived mind allowed me to remain in a kind of suspended animation. When we left the mountains and hit the main highway on the Andalusia flatlands, my overworked brain gave up trying to keep me even half-awake, and I joined the girls in exhausted slumber.

I came awake when the sound of the SUV's engine died, and I realized we had come to a stop and Liza was saying, "Is anyone hungry?"

A little embarrassed that I had fallen asleep, I pretended that I had been awake all the time by

150

practically leaping out of the SUV. I discovered that we had stopped at one of the roadside rest areas unique to European freeways. Restaurants, shops and rest rooms were situated in a structure that arched over the highway like a huge bridge. Gas stations were on the ground on both sides of the structure. All the shops clinging to the huge bridge looked neat and clean with all their signs and directions in both Spanish and English. Some signs were even augmented with German, Italian and one or more mysterious languages.

Pepe had stopped in a parking area near a restaurant that had the look of an American fast-food chain. Liza opened the SUV's doors and the girls slowly climbed out where they stood blinking and rubbing their eyes as they looked around.

"Are we there?" Valarie asked.

"Where are we?" Dawn said as she yawned and stretched. The picture of Dawn stretching with her hands raised high drove all sleep from my eyes.

Liza said, "We're about half-way. You'd better use the restroom. Then come to the restaurant."

"Which way are the restrooms?" Heather said.

Pepe pointed. "*Allí.* There, Señorita."

A few minutes later when Pepe and I were washing our hands in the men's room, he said, "Señor Calvin, did you notice the yellow car?"

His words drove away my last vestiges of sleep. "Yellow car? No. Did you see one?"

"When we left Granada. And once later, near Bailen." He saw the look on my face and shrugged, "I'm not sure it was the same one."

He was probably right. There had to be a lot of little yellow cars in Spain. But the thought that the

151

paparazzi might be following us kept me wide-eyed and glancing back over my shoulder all during the remainder of the long drive to Madrid. I didn't see any sign of a yellow car, but that didn't mean they weren't back there somewhere out of sight. The time to watch for them was in Madrid when they would have to stay close to keep from losing us in the traffic.

But although I kept a wary eye out until we arrived at our hotel, I didn't spot any yellow car, nor any sign of the two goons. I began to relax with the knowledge that there were hundreds of hotels in Madrid so even if they had managed to trail us into the city, once we were lost in the labyrinth of streets, parks, and passageways, the chances of them finding us was about one in a million.

One nice thing about arriving in Madrid late in the evening was that it was too late to visit any museums, cathedrals or castles.

By the time we were all settled in it was after ten o'clock. Pepe had gone to his home and we were having dinner at a restaurant that the hotel's concierge suggested. We had been lucky to get a table situated on the sidewalk on the edge of a public plaza surrounded by trees, restaurants, apartment buildings and shops. It was a lovely plaza paved with tile in intricate patterns with a bubbling fountain in the center. Although it was nearing eleven p.m. the plaza was practically teeming with people. Many, occupying picnic-like tables and benches, were families who paid no attention to children of all ages playing in the plaza. There was, of course, music provided by a strolling group of musicians with violins, guitars and the accordion. There were even clowns and jugglers. I would not have been surprised to hear a couple of opera singers.

Some of the little kids were really good dancers. Imitating flamenco dancers, the boys, with their hands on their hips, strutted and stomped their feet and the girls twirled and waved their arms. And when the music changed to salsa almost everyone, young and old, joined in the dancing. Strangely, unlike the *tapas* bars, there were not many young men or girls.

The girls noticed it, too, and were not thrilled with the situation.

"We want to go to some of those *tapa* places," Valerie said, "where we can dance."

"Okay," I agreed. "After dinner. But what you're seeing here is the real Spain. Even the kids don't go to bed before midnight."

"We still want to dance," Maria pouted.

The music had changed to a lively samba and some of the older people were also dancing. On an impulse I got up and offered my hand to Liza. "Come on, Liza," I said. "Let's show them how it's done."

To my surprise she got up, and after she'd taken a few steps out on the terrazzo plaza, she turned and held out her arms and wiggled her hips.

The gesture was so seductive I suppressed a gasp of surprise, but I did practically leap to meet her.

With no gigolos available, the girls got up and danced as a group. Caught up by the lively music they wiggled their hips and clapped their hands, imitating the moves of the children.

I, too was quickly seduced by the music's mesmerizing beat, and when the musicians segued into a fantastic fandango, I thought I was doing pretty well waving my arms, snapping my fingers and banging my feet on the terrazzo like castanets. In fact,

153

some people stopped dancing and started gathering around to watch, clapping their hands to the beat of the music. But they weren't looking at me. It was Liza. The music had pulled her into a frenzied fandango with her hair flailing, her skirt flying, her hands twining above her head and her feet moving like a demented gazelle. Even the musicians got caught up in her dance because they moved in close so they could play just for her. All I had to do was stand aside and stomp my feet and clap my hands once in a while because nobody was looking at me.

It was a good thing I wasn't too caught up in the dance because I appeared to be the only one in the plaza who noticed two men standing off to the side who were not watching Liza's dancing. Instead, their concentration was on Heather and Dawn who were dancing together on the outskirts of the crowd. When the two men moved out of the shadows toward the girls I stopped dancing. They were Bruno and Simon and they were edging toward Heather and Dawn, and I didn't see a sign of a camera.

I tried to force my way through the crowd to intercept them, but the crowd was packed too tight. The two would reach the unsuspecting girls long before I could, and I had no doubt they meant to grab them.

I called the girl's names but my voice was lost in the din of the music and the hand clapping.

Then the two goons made a mistake: they shoved a couple of children out of their path, and I saw my chance. I pointed at them and yelled, "Molesta! Molesta! Molesta del ninos!"

It was as though I'd cut the music off with a sharp knife. I mean it stopped in the middle of a note

154

and everyone instantly turned, their heads swiveling, their eyes wide with alarm. Some woman saw one of the little girls getting to her feet and the two strangers standing over her and she picked up the scent, pointing at the two goons and yelling, "Perverte! Perverte!"

Yelling invectives, the entire crowd charged the two men who stood stricken with amazement. Then both began backing up, saying, "No. No."

Too late. The crowd with women in the front, began pummeling the two with fists, purses, shoes, whatever they could lay their hands on. Cowering, covering their heads with their arms, the two men turned and ran, scrambling between buildings using passageways too narrow for the crowd to follow.

Giving up the chase, women and men quickly gathered their children and returned to their tables, babbling about 'pervertes.'

The musicians began playing again. But it was no use: the mood had been destroyed and no one wanted to dance. The ladies and I decided to try getting the mood back for our group by ordering more *Mahou* for them and grape juice for me. For once, even the girls were quiet.

I was grateful for the chance to think. The fact that the two knew where to find us not only puzzled me, it tightened an iron band of worry around my brain. Even if Pepe had seen their yellow car following us on the drive from Ronda, I was sure they could not have found us once we hit the dense traffic in Madrid. We were not even staying at the same hotel where we'd stayed before.

All the facts seemed to point to the conclusion that someone had told them. I knew now they weren't

155

simply paparazzi looking for pictures of American girls touring Spain. They were after the golden girl. But if so, who was keeping them informed of our location? Liza? One of the girls? Why would they? I'm sure that, except for the golden girl herself, none of them were even aware there was a billionaire among them. And so far, golden girl hadn't dropped a clue. I was even beginning to suspect that Mr. Kimberly's entire story was a pack of lies that the two goons had brought just as I had. Except, why would he lie? What would be the point? And why would he lie to me? I was low man on our glamorous totem pole. And I sure wasn't some kind of body guard who could overpower a bunch of potential kidnappers single-handed. I probably couldn't even overpower one. Although I had handled that stupido on the dance floor pretty well. But that ape Bruno was a horse of a different color.

Then there was Pepe. What did we really know about him? Only that this was his first time working for Kimberly Tours. Had Mr. Kimberly taken him into his confidence about the golden girl? I rather doubted it. What would be the point? Then, too, Pepe had told me about the yellow car following us. Besides, I just couldn't bring myself to believe he could not be trusted.

And the paparazzis themselves. I knew now they weren't really photographers? But how did they know that one of the girls was megarich, even if they didn't know which on?

Oh, Lordy, Lordy. What had I gotten myself into this time?

My cogitations were interrupted by Liza saying to me, "Those two men. Weren't they the same ones taking pictures of us in Seville?"

I was going to say no, but decided she would know I was lying, so I said, "I think so. The paparazzi. You wouldn't think they were child molesters."

Judging from her expression I rather doubted that she thought they were. "I think they were stalking us," she said. "When they pushed those kids it was just to get closer to us."

I pretended to consider that for a second. I didn't want to alarm her by asking the obvious question, then decided she was probably asking herself, so I said, "How do you suppose they found us?"

"How indeed?" The way she looked at me when she said it made me wonder if she considered me a suspect.

I tried to assuage her suspicions. "Pepe said he saw their yellow car following us on the highway."

But she was no fool. "Even if they had been following us," she said. "I don't see how they could follow us to the hotel in all that traffic. I didn't see them when we checked in."

"Me neither. Maybe after tonight they'll leave us alone."

"I hope so. I've got enough to worry about."

But judging by the way she pressed her lips together in a thin, hard line made me believe she didn't really believe we'd seen the last of them.

But then, neither did I.

I gave up trying to solve the puzzle. We were halfway through the tour, and so far nothing bad had happened. All I had to do was keep those two goons away from us for another few days and we'd be home free.

I relaxed with my glass of grape juice and smiled

at Liza and the girls who were giggling over something one of them had said about perverts. Tomorrow we would finish the run up to Pamplona, catch that running-of-the-bulls fiesta, then see what Pamplona had in the way of night life. Easy. There was even the thought of a nude beach.

CHAPTER 16

My optimistic faith in the old Dorsey luck started to come apart the next day when we were all settled in the SUV, zipping along about a hundred miles north of Madrid on our way to Pamplona.

According to my map Pamplona is north of Madrid, not too far from the Bay of Biscay so we should be on some main highway taking us north to a big city called Zaragoza, then north-west to Pamplona. But the road we were on didn't seem like a major highway. Not that I was complaining. Madrid is situated on kind of a high plateau where the surrounding country is fairly dry, almost desert, kind of like Arizona. But traveling north, we had gradually moved into country with more hills and valleys, more greenery: forests, grass, brush. The farther north we went the more the topography reminded me of pictures I'd seen of Switzerland.

Staring out the SUV's window at the lovely views, I had lost my desire to sleep. I was, however, a little concerned that we seemed to have left the main four lane highway and were traveling on a narrow two lane road. But I supposed Pepe knew what he was doing. One good thing, with so few cars or trucks on the road it was easy to keep a lookout behind us for the yellow car. But the road was deserted, at least as far as I could see. In fact, a little too deserted for my peace of mind.

And that was the good news.

It has always been a source of amazement to me how fast my life can go from fair to bad. It never seems to work the other way around.

159

I was reminded of this again when the SUV suddenly lurched and the girls, shocked wide awake, screamed in terror as the SUV careened to the other side of the highway before Pepe could muscle it back to the right lane. Fortunately, the highway was deserted and Pepe was able to pull to the shoulder and stop.

If there had been traffic in the other lane we could have had a catastrophic crash, so I guess the old Dorsey luck had kicked in in the nick of time.

"What is it?" Dawn yelped. "What happened?"

I said, "Tire. Blowout. Nothing to worry about."

Anyone who knows how to drive a car knows what a blowout is, even if it had never happened to them. So the girls pretty well took it in stride, and settled down to resume their naps.

When Liza and I got out with Pepe we could see that it was the left front tire. Pepe knelt and ran his hands over the tread.

"*Mira*," he said. "A bolt."

Kneeling beside him I saw the head of a small bolt protruding from the tire. It was big enough to cause the tire to suddenly lose pressure, which could have cost our lives if it had happened on the main highway. Of course, on the main highway there probably weren't any bolts lying around.

"Where's the spare?" I said to Pepe. "I'll help you change it."

Pepe stood up and sort of shrugged his shoulders with his hands spread as though he was going to give us some bad news. Of course, I was right.

"No spare," he said.

"No spare?" Liza sort of gasped. "Why not?"

Pepe's smile was rueful. "I need money."

160

"You sold it?" Liza almost shouted. "You came on this trip with no spare tire?"

"No *problema*," Pepe said. "There is station in Soria. They fix it."

I said, "How do we get to this station with no tire?"

Pepe scratched his head. "Walk, *por supuesto*."

"How long will that take?" Liza said.

Pepe shrugged. *"No si."*

Liza sort of clinched her teeth. "The bulls run at eight in the morning. That means we've got to be in Pamplona tonight."

Pepe said, "*No problema?* Maybe car or truck come by and give a ride."

"And if it doesn't?"

"We get there later. *No problema.*"

Liza kind of rolled her eyes before she closed them, looking a little weary, but she said nothing.

I had been checking out the highway and the nearby hills. Not a car, truck or house in sight. Where were those paparazzis when you needed them?

"Why are we out here?" I asked. "This isn't the main highway."

"How you say...shortcut."

"Shortcut," Liza snarled. "We should have stayed on the main highway."

Pepe lifted an eyebow. "You tell Pepe you in big hurry. So I take shortcut."

"Well, this certainly isn't saving any time," Liza countered.

Since the milk was already spilled, I said, "Well, let's get this tire off. I'll help you."

"You do have a jack?" Liza said as though she doubted it.

"Oh, sure," Pape smiled. "*Gato*, wrench, *todo. No problema.*"

We had to unload the bags before we could get at the jack and lug-bolt wrench. The girls watched anxiously as we piled their bags on the dirt shoulder of the road.

I had changed enough tires on my own old cars to know exactly what to do, so Pepe and I quickly had the SUV jacked up and the flat tire off. The rusty bolt that **had done** the damage looked to **be about half an** inch in diameter. Pepe was going to try to pull it out of the tire, but I convinced him to leave it in place so a mechanic could easily locate the puncture and, also, know the size of the hole. I hoped Pepe had enough Spanish dinero with him to buy another tire if this one couldn't be repaired.

After we had the tire off, I looked up at the sun and gave Pepe a pat on the shoulder. "Better get started, Pepe. We're running out of time."

"Si," Pepe said. "*No problema.*" He tilted the tire upright so he could roll it.

Liza said, "Wait. You can't leave us here."

Pepe looked as startled as I suddenly felt. Somehow I knew this was not going to work out well for me.

Pepe sort of gazed around at the deserted hills. "*Porque no*? Why not?"

"Alone? In this...wilderness. We don't even speak the language. What if something happens?"

Pepe knit his heavy eyebrows in puzzled consternation. "But, *Señorita*, I have to take *la lanta*, the tire..."

"No you don't."

Pepe's puzzle expression deepened. "I don't?"

"Calvin can take it."

There it was. Once again the sword of Damacles was about to punch a hole in my innocent head.

Pepe's eyes swiveled to look at me. Then they lifted as though it suddenly dawned on him that he might not have to walk about a hundred miles rolling a tire. He said, "*Señor Calvin. Si.* Pepe will stay here and guard the *señoritas.*"

"Wait a minute," I said. "I don't know where this tire place is. I can guard the ladies."

Liza's eyes seemed to compare my lean, athletic body to Pepe blocky bulk. But to her credit, she didn't mention our physics. Instead, she said, "How can you guard us? You don't even speak Spanish."

I would have felt better if she'd left that word 'even' out of her remark, but I still had the sinking feeling that I was doomed even if I spoke fluent Spanish or Chinese or Russian, even ancient Arabic. I looked at Pepe. "How far is this place?"

His grin was so broad I could see that he had a couple of gold-filled molars. "*No mucho distencia,*" he said. "Five kilometers, maybe."

I made some mental calculations. A kilometer was six-tenths of a mile. So ten kilometers would be six miles. Five kilometers then would be half that or three miles. Only three miles? I jogged more than that.

"Okay," I said. "I'll do it. But I'll need some dinero."

Moving fast, as though she was afraid I'd change my mind, Liza hauled her purse out of the SUV and shoved a handful of paper money in my hand. "Here," she said. "Get a receipt."

I was too disgusted at my bad luck to even say goodbye as I set off along the deserted road, rolling the

163

tire. The way things turned out I should have said 'farewell.'

For one thing the road meandered up and down like a rollercoaster, and I discovered that rolling a tire uphill can be hard work, but rolling it down hill could be disastrous. On even the most shallow slope the tire would take off like it wanted to escape, and I had to chase it until it careened off the road and plowed through grass and bushes until it hit a tree or boulder that killed it. Then I had to plow back through the grass and bushes and wrestle it onto the road where it rolled along patiently until the next hill. I soon realized that the only way to outwit the malevolent beast on a downward slope, was to pick it up and carry it. Which did not help either my temperament or my clothing.

At the end of what I thought was about three miles, I discovered that the little 'maybe' Pepe had added at the end of his five kilometers should have raised my suspicion because there was no sign of a city, or even a house.

A short time later I considered being pelted by a brief rainstorm to be icing on my cake of woe. After all, it could have been a tornado or a snowstorm, even being swept away by a tsunami wouldn't have surprised me.

I suppose the tire protection gods were growing bored with tormenting me because before I perished on the side of the road I was able to flag down a ride from a passing truck.

The truck driver—who spoke a little English— also knew a place on the edge of the next little town that repaired tires. But more bad news: the tire was beyond repair and the mechanic—with the truck driver translating—said he did not have another in stock.

164

Tomorrow he would drive to Zaragosa to get one. Pamplona, he explained, was closer, but it would be so jammed with tourists for the Fiesta de San Fermen it would be impossible to obtain a new tire there. Meanwhile, we could all stay overnight at the only hotel in town.

One good thing: the mechanic gave me a ride back to our SUV where the four girls almost had a fit of snickering when they saw me in my damp, dirty clothes.

I thought Liza took the news pretty well that we probably would not be in Pamplona in the morning for the running of the bulls. To her credit, she even helped me drag my bag from the SUV and made the girls turn their backs while I changed clothes. She actually produced a huge comb from somewhere and used it on my hair. It was not an easy task. My hair, that I wear fashionably long, had dried in place after the wind in the rainstorm had tousled it willy-nilly, and while I was grateful for her help, I had to grit my teeth to keep from yelling with pain as she forced the comb through my nature-created dreadlocks.

I discovered the reason for her ruthless behavior when she muttered, "We'll never make it. We'll never make it now."

"Make what?"

"The running of the bulls. Tomorrow morning is the last day."

I checked my watch. Although the sun was still hanging above the horizon, it was almost 7:00 p.m., and I figured we could reach Pamplona in a couple of hours if we could get a ride.

"I'll talk to the mechanic," I said. "Maybe he'll take us."

165

I was rewarded by a dazzling smile. "Oh. Good idea. You think he will?"

"I'll find out." I walked to the rear of the SUV where Pepe and the mechanic were loading our bags into the truck.

"Pepe," I said. "Ask him if he'll take us all the way to Pamplona. We'll pay him, of course."

Pepe rubbed his chin, then smiled. "Bueno." He turned to the mechanic. "Señor,..." He rattled off something in Spanish and the mechanic looked at him like he was crazy before he rattled something back.

Pepe turned to me. "He said only a loco or a fool would go anywhere near Pamplona during fiesta."

I thought how Liza would take the news, and I rubbed my thumb over my fingers in the ancient sign meaning money. "Dinero," I said. "Mucho dinero."

The mechanic shook his head, and said one of the few words I knew in Spanish. It was 'no.' He added a few words I was kind of glad I didn't understand, but I got the message.

I went to tell Liza, but I really didn't have to translate when she saw my expression. "He won't do it," she said.

"Right. I even offered him a lot of money, but he still won't do it."

She took a deep breath. "All right. We'll have to stay in that place until the tire is fixed. As for the running of the bulls,"---her eyes got that intense look I had come to fear---"I'll think of something."

Remembering the look in her eyes, I was slowly turning into a nervous wreck by the time the mechanic had towed the SUV into the small city of Soria and we were settled in a picturesque hotel. Like eagles locating gophers, the girls had found one of the ubiquitous

166

tapas bars with its requisite accordion and guitar players.

After our by now habitual 10:00 p.m. dinner, the girls were up dancing with each other or whatever males they could find, before I could work up enough courage to broach the bull-running subject to Liza.

"Uh...this running of the bulls. I don't think the ladies even know what it is. If we can locate some *tapas* that open early, they won't miss it."

She turned her eyes on me as though I had interrupted some deep introspection. "Yes, they will," she said. "It's in the contract."

There it was again: the four little words that made my heart stop. "But the tire blew out. Pepe sold the spare. That's not our fault."

"In a way it is. Pepe is a Kimberly employee. That makes us responsible."

"Well, if you look at it that way..."

She glanced around the room. "Where is Pepe? I'd like to talk to him."

"I think he's at the hotel where he could keep an eye on the SUV. He feels responsible."

"He should." She got up. "I'm going to talk to him. There's got to be a way we can get to Pamplona early in the morning."

She started toward the door and in a moment of panic I called, "Wait!" When she stopped and looked back, I said. "The check here. I don't have any money."

"I'll be back," she said. "Keep an eye on the girls."

She headed for the door, and I slumped in my chair. How did I get myself in this mess? With Bruno and his partner on the loose there was no telling what

167

they might do. Keep an eye on the girls indeed. I couldn't even go to the bathroom.

CHAPTER 17

I was awakened the next morning by the ringing of my cell phone. Rubbing the sleep out of my eyes, I looked at my watch: 11:00. It was probably 11:00 a.m., although judging by my weary bones after not getting to bed until around 3:00 in the morning, it could easily have been 11:00 p.m. The sun filtering into my curtained window, however, was another clue that it wasn't approaching midnight.

I answered the phone with a voice that was not much more than a croak. As I suspected, it was Liza.

"Are you up?" she asked.

I laughed, or I tried to laugh; what came out was more of a groan. "Up? Are you kidding? I'm lucky to be alive."

I hadn't really expected much sympathy from her, and sure enough, there was none in her voice when she said, "The last running of the bulls in Pamplona was at eight this morning. We missed it. I just knew we would."

For some unknown reason I felt a little sorry for her. She had put this entire tour together like a fine watch, and at every turn it had betrayed her. Thus far she had managed to pull the roast out of the fire, but there wasn't anything she could do this time. The de San Fermin festival people in Pamplona certainly weren't going to schedule an additional bull run. They probably wouldn't even do it for the Pope let alone for little old Kimberly Tours.

But then again, they weren't dealing with Liza Barlow.

"Get up," she said. "I've arranged for a running

of the bulls right after lunch. Two p.m."

I had to swallow a large dose of astonishment before I could say, "You have? We'll never make it to Pamplona by two o'clock."

"Not Pamplona. Here."

"Here?" My voice practically hit a high C. "Here?" I repeated.

"That's right. Get ready. I'll get the girls up."

She hung up, and I sat frozen with a mixture of disbelief and dread. Somehow these schemes of hers always seemed to bode disaster for Calvin Dorsey.

As it turned out, I didn't know the half of it.

After we'd finished brunch Liza pulled me aside from the four somnambulistic girls who seemed to take it for granted that they would be witnessing the famous running of the bulls. I don't know whether they were surprised to find that it would be occurring here in the little town of Soria instead of in Pamplona, or they were too zonked from last night to even realize where they were.

"Here's the situation," Liza told me. "I've talked to the mayor and some of the town officials and they were very cooperative. You might say they were delighted to think we might be starting some sort of tradition for Soria. They're cordoning off a street for the run."

"But the bulls," I said. "Where are you going to get a flock of bulls? They don't grow on trees."

"Pepe is taking care of that."

"And the people they'll be chasing? Where are you going to round up people crazy enough to run in front of a bunch of bulls that would like nothing better than to skewer them on their horns?"

"Exactly," she said. "You'll have to fill in."

170

My eyes wanted to blink in surprise, but my brain knew better. What surprise? It has seen this coming. I don't know why the rest of my body could be so stupid. Maybe it was trying to pretend it wasn't about to be paraded through the streets of Soria in little pieces dangling from the horns of a herd of killer bulls.

"Me?" I managed to say. "It would be a great honor, I'm sure, to be the first one killed at the famous Soria running of the bulls, but it's an honor I could do without, thank you."

"Nonsense," Liza said. "If a bull gets close you just play dead. They run right past."

"PLAY dead? More likely I would be dead. Don't you know people have actually been killed?"

"Not since nineteen-sixty-something. I read up on it."

"Well, I don't want to break the record. I'm not going to do it."

"You have to. It's in your contract."

"Well, I quit. So sue me."

She sat staring at me with the lovely, deadly eyes. "Calvin," she said. "I'm really surprised. I didn't take you for a coward."

"Well, I am. A big living coward."

Tears gathered in her lovely, soulful eyes. "I see," she said. "Your word means nothing. What will your mother think?"

"My mother?"

"Of course." She reached over and put her hand over mine. "You'll have to tell her."

"Tell her what?"

"Tell her how you went back on your sworn promise, how you broke your word to do your duty."

I pictured the look on my mother's face when

171

she learned the truth, that I was a coward, that I had deserted my duty in the face of a little bodily harm. I would rather be dead, or at least slightly injured.

I sighed in resignation. "All right. But if one of those bulls tries to spear me he's going to have to catch me."

"Of course. That's why they call it the running of the bulls."

I was surprised at how quickly the tears in her eyes had dried up. She glanced at her watch. "You'd better get changed. See if you can find some white clothes. It seems to be a tradition for the runners. Something about showing the blood better, I suppose."

I was thinking about that as I dug a white shirt out of my bag while thinking it would be better if I had a red shirt so the blood wouldn't be so obvious, at least to me.

As a tribute to tradition, I did tie a red bandana around my neck, but I was almost in a state of panic until I found my old tennis shoes. I used to be a pretty good runner, and wearing the light-weight tennis shoes should give me a fighting chance.

My confidence was ebbing fast, however, after Liza had introduced me to the town mayor and the village priest who gave me a blessing that seemed suspiciously like last rites.

We were standing at the beginning of a narrow cobble stoned street that kind of zigzagged through an old part of town and was closely hemmed in by two and three story apartments, all painted rusty brown. Side streets had been blocked off with sawhorses to confine the bulls to the main street. At least, I think they were for the bulls. Maybe they were supposed to keep the runners (me) from escaping. Well, think

172

again, bull-lovers. Those sawhorses might intimidate a bull, but if some bull was breathing on my neck a cement wall wouldn't stop me.

"Calvin," someone called. "Is that you?"

I looked toward the sound of the voice. The four girls were standing on a second floor balcony of a building waving at me. I waved back, but their waves, instead of waves of greeting or good luck, looked more like waves of goodbye. It made me wonder if they would like to see the bulls catch up with me under their balcony where they would have a good view. The fact that they all had their cameras ready made me a little suspicious. Somehow I doubted they were for selfies.

My attention shifted back to the street when I heard the snuffling of bulls in the barricade behind me at the beginning of the run.

Pepe apparently had been successful in rounding up a herd of killer bulls. The sounds from the impatient behemoths increased, and the mayor and the priest hurried away. Even Liza began edging for an open doorway as she told me, "Keep to the middle of the street. Try to make it to the end. It'll be good advertising."

"How far is the end?" I asked.

"Not far. A few blocks. Good luck."

She ducked out the side door, slamming it shut behind her, and I thought I heard a heavy bolt being closed. I glanced at the barricade behind me. There was a kind of makeshift gate built in where I assumed the bulls would emerge, and I moved up to give myself a longer head start. At the sound behind me of a bolt being forced open, my heart beat began thudding so hard I could feel the blood coursing through my veins as though it was fully aware of what soon was going to

173

happen to it. I crouched ready to launch myself into action.

But it wasn't the barricade gate that crashed open. It was the door. And it wasn't Liza who came charging out, ready to rescue me. It was Bruno and Simon!

Simon said, "So, there you are. We're gonna kick your---"

That was as far as he got. Behind me the barricade gate slammed open and six bulls charged through on a dead run, their heads lowered and their tiny, immature horns aimed at my posterior. Tiny? Immature?

They weren't huge, savage brutes; they were calves! But big calves! Calves with short but pointy horns and slashing hooves!

I bolted out of my crouch faster than James Bolt coming out of the blocks. No bull, full grown or just a big calf, was going to catch Calvin Dorsey!

I could have walked. There were cries of terror behind me as six bulls slammed into Bruno and Simon!

I slowed to see who was winning.

Bad move.

Bruno and Simon, their legs churning and their arms pumping, were almost on top of me with the six bulls gaining on them, their heads down, trying to impale the two paparazzi on their immature horns.

With a startled yelp I leaped into full fled. With me holding a good lead, we passed under the balcony where the four girls and Liza shouted encouragement, to whom I wasn't sure.

Down the street we charged. If Paul Revere had been ridding his horse down that street we would have passed him. Or I would have. Bruno and Simon were not quite so lucky. Simon, his legs churning, was holding his own ahead of the charging bulls, but Bruno's lumbering gait didn't have a chance. The bulls were gaining on him nicely and sheer panic gave him such a burst of speed that he charged up Simon's back and they both went down in a tangle of arms, legs, and swear words.

The bulls loved it. They not only ran over the pair, they paused to try out their sprouting horns, then wheeled back to practice the bull-rage they would someday vent on matadors in the bull ring.

But Simon and Bruno's bad luck was my good luck. While the bulls expended their innate savagery on Bruno and Simon, I was able to gain a huge lead. I barely noticed crowds of cheering people on balconies and behind barricaded side streets as I streaked past.

When I reached a barricade at the far end of the street, I'd probably broken the world's record for the three-block dash. Then I topped it off by probably breaking the high-jump record. I know my stupendous leap cleared the barricade by a good three feet. I kept on running for another ten or fifteen seconds. I don't know how far I managed to run in those few seconds, but after I finally stopped I had gone so far it took me about half an hour to walk back.

CHAPTER 18

I was still wearing my un-bloodied bull-running clothes and had pretty well recovered the use of my arms, legs and lungs when some time later I accompanied Liza and the girls to one of Soria's *tapas* bars. Even though it was midmorning, the bar was doing a great business with people celebrating the city's first ever running of the bulls. Not only was it a first for the running, it was the first for putting two Americans in the hospital with multiple cuts and bruises, none of which proved to be life threatening. But I was sure Simon and Bruno did not consider it a great honor. Fortunately, none of the bulls had been injured.

While I was sitting at a table near the crowded dance floor, the town mayor and other dignitaries as well as several villagers stopped by to congratulate me for making their little town famous.

I accepted their congratulations graciously, but actually, I didn't feel much like a hero. I tried to convince myself that I had managed to survive the running of the bulls due to my athletic prowess, but I knew I'd probably only survived because of Simon and Bruno's ill-timed intervention. On the other hand, I had run so well that if push had come to shove, I didn't believe those bulls could ever have caught me.

The point being that after I convinced myself I really was a hero, I was able to accept their congratulations with the proper nonchalant panache.

During a break in the adulations, Liza said, "I don't understand how they keep finding us. Soria isn't on our schedule. If they somehow got hold of our

176

itinerary, they should have been waiting in Pamplona."

"That's right," I agreed. "I don't think they were following us. On those deserted roads, we would have seen them."

"So somebody's telling them." She glanced toward the dance floor where the girls were bouncing like demented dervishes. "But who?"

"Do the ladies even know our itinerary?"

"They should. It's in their travel agreement. But I don't think they'd tell. They don't like those paparazzis any more than we do.""

I also couldn't believe it was one of the girls, but that only left one other person. "Pepe," I said. "It has to be Pepe."

She shook her head. "I don't believe it. Not Pepe. He wouldn't do that."

"So how do they know?"

"My guess is somebody at the agency."

"The agency? Kimberly?"

She nodded. "Mr. Kimberly wanted to keep it as confidential as possible. I guess it was because he was afraid something like this would happen. But I guess somebody in the agency found out about it. They must get paid to tell."

"Makes sense. Paparazzis probably smelled money in four American college girls touring in Europe."

She began to nod, then broke into a snigger. "I'll bet this morning they wished they'd kept their money."

I had to laugh also. "I'll bet this afternoon they wish it even more."

She nodded and laughed again. I was suddenly struck by how seldom I'd seen her laugh, and I couldn't believe how much it changed her. Throughout our trip it seemed as though her face had usually been drawn by worry. She had still been lovely, but loveliness etched with deep concern is not the same as happy lovely.

Even now her happy mood didn't last long.

When the musicians took a break the girls trooped back to the table and resumed sipping their sherry or Mahou.

"Did you see the guy dancing with me," Heather **said. "He was drop dead handsome."**

"Yes, but he was a lousy dancer," Valerie said.

"Who cares," Heather answered. "I just wanted to look at him."

"Most of the guys are not that good," Dawn said. "Not like Seville or Madrid."

"No wonder," Maria said. "These guys work for a living. I think all those guys in Madrid were gigolos."

"Gigolo. What's a gigolo?" Heather asked.

"A guy who lives off women."

Dawn laughed. "We've got plenty of those back home."

"And they're all great dancers," Maria said. "That's how you can tell."

"Or when they invite you to dinner and expect you to pick up the check," Dawn said.

Valerie turned to Liza, "What about Barcelona? Do they have *tapas* where they dance?"

Liza kind of waved aside the question. "Every place in Spain has tapas where they dance."

I recognized a chance to bolster my credentials. "Barcelona is supposed to have more tapa bars than any place in Spain."

"Wonderful," Valerie said.

Dawn made her hands into fists "Oh, good."

178

Maria looked at me. "How soon will we be there?"

"Well, let me see." I glanced at my watch. "It's only eleven o'clock now. If Pepe has the car ready, we can leave right away. We should be there in time for dinner."

Dawn's smile with her perfect teeth, made my heart double its beat. "I don't care if they are gigolos," she said. "I like the way they dance."

"Do they have shops," Maria interjected. "Lots of shops."

"Of course" Liza turned to me. "Calvin, tell them about Barcelona." She smiled at me, a kind of 'Go-ahead. Make-a-fool-of-yourself' smile.

I practically leaped to the challenge. "Barcelona?" What had I read about Barcelona? I had no idea. I had to make up something. Something plausible. The girls wouldn't know I was making it up. Even Liza said she'd never been there. "A big city," I began "Very...uh...modern. Lots of tapas. And a...ah...castle...a royal castle." That sounded good. Every Spanish city had a castle. "Very unique. It's called the...the.." A picture popped into my head. "Big, with towering spires. Built by a famous architect named...uh... starts with a G."

"Gucci," Dawn said. "I like his shoes."

"He's Italian," Heather said.

"And he designs clothes and bags," Valerie added. "Not shoes."

I noticed that Liza was staring at me with her doubtful expression. "Are you sure?" she asked.

The doubt dripping from her voice made me certain I would have gotten it wrong if she had asked me my name. "Uh," I said. "Well, yeah. He also built a

179

couple of funny looking houses."

"Oh, Goudi," she said, with a lot of superciliousness in her voice. "You're thinking of Antonio Goudi."

Oh, oh. She had probably been reading the tourist guides. Well, two could play at that game. "Right," I said. "He also made that castle with the tall spires."

She kind of groaned before she said, "It's not a castle. It's a church. A cathedral."

Fortunately, Valerie said, "I've seen enough cathedrals."

"Me too," Dawn said. "What else have they got?"

"Well...," Frantically I searched my mind for data. "A seaport," I almost shouted. "On the Mediterranean. Ships, boats, yachts. Lots of yachts."

"Yachts?" Dawn said. "I love yachts."

"We're not going on any yachts," Liza said. "You can see yachts at home."

"Castles," I said, clutching at straws. You can't go wrong about castles. Not in Spain. "They've got lots of castles, really big castles, where kings and queens live."

"Pooie," Maria said. "I've seen enough castles."

"Wait a minute," Heather said. "What about the beach? We're supposed to go to a beach. I remember. It's in our contract."

I leaped at the opening. "Right. Beaches. Barcelona is famous for it's beaches." I looked at Liza. She was sort of biting her lower lip like she was not too happy about the mention of beaches, so I quickly added. "Uh. Probably."

"I remember," Maria interjected. "Not just any

180

beach. A nude beach."

Heather's eyes popped wide. "That's right," she agreed. "A nude beach."

At the thought of the four---no five---lovelies on a nude beach my mind went into overdrive. "Right," I yelped. "A nude beach. All day long."

Heather turned to Liza. "Isn't that's right, Liza? It's in the contract?"

Liza sort of growled in her throat and the look she turned on me said it was all my fault. "I'm not sure," she said. "I...forgot about that."

I knew that was a lie. She'd probably seen the look in my eyes when a nude beach was mentioned that had made her wishing the girls had forgotten it.

"No," Heather insisted. "I remember. Costa something."

"That's it," Maria said. "Costa Dorada. A nude beach."

Dawn glanced at me, her eyes sparkling with mischief, "Men too?" she asked.

All eyes suddenly were directed at me with messages ranging from expectation to skepticism to dismay.

My own face reflected stunned rejection. "Men? No, no. Only girls. Pretty girls."

Liza saw my look and smiled her evil smile. "I think she's right. It is in the contract."

I didn't know whether to jump for joy or start looking for an escape. I was more than ready to see my travel companions running around *au natural*? And was I ready for them to see me? No way, Jose.

Liza saved me from hyperventilating by saying, "Most are not really nude. They're more clothing optional."

Clothing optional? Well, that put a new light on it, a lovely light. I could wear my bathing trunks, while the girls.... I shied away from the mental image in time to prevent embarrassment. "The castle," I said. "Forget the beach. Too much sand. Gritty sand. You'll love the royal castle."

"A vote," Valerie said while staring at me as though wondering how much money I would bring on eBay. "What is it, girls? Some old castle or the nude beach?"

The other ladies said, "The beach," so quickly my lone vote for the castle got lost in the cacophony.

Liza looked a little nonplussed until her gaze turned to me and she smiled that increasingly familiar snide smile that froze my heart. "I guess it's the beach," she said.

"Right," Heather agreed. "I wonder how all those gigolos will look with no clothes."

The gigolos? Of course. They had to be somewhere in the daylight. Why not the beach? Given a choice, the ladies wouldn't be looking at me. I was saved.

From the look in her eyes the mental picture of handsome men on a nude beach had caused Liza's depression to disappear. Then I realized she was still staring at me with that malevolent smile, and I realized it's hard to look depressed when one is trying to keep from laughing one's head off.

CHAPTER 19

According to my map, Coasta Dorada was only a few miles south of Barcelona. But it was almost 200 miles from Soria so, even though most of the way we would use the main highway from Zaragosa, it would still take hours to reach the coast.

It couldn't be too soon for me. Just the thought of lounging under an umbrella in my baggy bathing suit with a root-beer float in one hand and a pair of binoculars in the other while the four girls cavorted in the warm Mediterranean waves made me wish we had a helicopter instead of a slow SUV.

There was another good thing: by spending as much time as possible at the beach, I wouldn't have to take the girls on a tour of Barcelona, at least not right away. That would give me time to read up on its major attractions. On the other hand, if I saw the four ladies on a nude beach, I probably wouldn't be wasting time reading about famous sights in Barcelona or anywhere else on earth.

But after lunch I'd learned from a quick perusal of my guide books that Coasta Dorada was not a city. It was an area of the Mediterranean coast south of Barcelona that covered about twenty miles and was famous for its gorgeous beaches. Lots of palm trees and sand.

I didn't know exactly where we'd be staying and didn't really care; that was Liza's responsibility. But I had to admit, the route Pepe took through Zaragoza to a place called Tarragona and on to the coast was a beautiful drive. We arrived in late afternoon and during the drive along the coast even the girls stayed awake, pointing out lovely sandy beaches and spectacular hotels.

When Pepe pulled the van up in the parking area of a three-story hotel that appeared to front directly on the beach, we quickly piled out of the SUV and stretched the kinks out of our legs.

Maria said to Liza, "Is this a nude beach? We're supposed to stay at a nude beach."

"That's what I understand," Liza said. "Clothing optional."

"Optional?" Valerie said. "That means we get to wear our bikinis."

"Only if we want to," Dawn said.

"Well," Maria said, "I didn't spend all that money on a bikini just to go naked."

It was a good thing I was able to take my mind off the lovely pictures building in my mind by helping Pepe unload the SUV while Liza led the chattering girls into the hotel.

Carrying a load of baggage, I found out why the parking area was in the rear of the hotel. The front entrance was up against a wide expanse of white sand dotted with poles supporting umbrellas made of palm fronds. Just beyond the beach the placid blue waters of a section of the Mediterranean I knew was called the Balearic Sea stretched to the horizon.

The beach, with its stretch of white sand and green palms, looked like something you'd find on a postcard, but I was a little disappointed in the Mediterranean. Pictures and movies I'd seen of beaches like Malibu in California always featured waves that crashed up on the beach in a constant rhythm, waves that were great for body or board surfing. But the Mediterranean surf was nothing but ripples that silently slid up on the beach a few feet like they were afraid any sound would destroy somebody's siesta. Well, it might not be great for surfing but it looked like I could swim all day without having to worry about a rip tide or undertow.

On the other hand, maybe that was why it was a clothing-optional beach. Since there was no playing in the waves, they had to invent some reason for people to come to the beach. Seeing naked people lounging around should do the trick. Although if the naked people were more than 30-years-old I think the sight of all those flabby bodies would drive more people away than attract them.

Even so I kept my eyes open for any clue that this might, indeed, be the promise land. I spotted a few people sitting in lounge chairs under umbrellas and a few others soaking up the afternoon sun by lying on towels on the sand. But everyone I could see wore a bathing suit.

That didn't appear portentous. I'd kind of expected the beach to be alive with beautiful girls *au naturel*, especially since the sand of the wide beach come right up to the front of the hotel where a number of round tables under umbrellas invited them.

On the other hand, remembering the looks the girls had given me, the sight of the tables gave me a sense of relief. This couldn't be a nude beach. Who could possibly be so narcissistic as to walk around in the nude in front of a bunch of diners. Especially if you were about 30 or 40, even 50. Talk about nauseating a good meal!

Unless...

A horrible thought struck me: suppose diners were also nude. I mean, if this really was a nude beach, where was the boundary? The sand came right up to the tables. Did the beach end there? Or did it extend into the hotel itself?

Then I noticed a couple of people seated at the hotel's beach-front tables, and, thank heavens, they had clothes on. A pair of bored looking waiters leaned against the building's façade and they also had their clothes on. That was reassuring, unless waiters were allowed to be exceptions. I certainly hoped so; I don't know about the girls, but being served by a nude male waiter would not have improved my appetite.

Entering the hotel I was wide-eyed, looking around anxiously. It was siesta time so there were only a few employees in the big lobby and, thank heavens, all had their clothes on.

After checking in, with little or no hope in finding shops open as yet, we all retired to our rooms with plans to meet for a little shopping before an early 9:00 p.m. dinner. That would get us started on sampling the area's night life at about 10:30 or 11:00, the perfect time to start an evening of nightclubbing. At least it was for me because it meant that in the morning the ladies would sleep late, maybe late enough so that when they hit the beach the sun would be nice and warm on their lovely bare bodies.

Actually, the plan worked out pretty well. When siesta time ended, my companions decided they would rather shop than hit the beach, even a nude beach. The fact that the sun was low on the horizon and twilight was cooling the sand also helped. But in preparation for tomorrow's hot sun, at the hotel's shop I bought a nice wide-brimmed straw hat.

I don't know if a hat was considered part of one's clothing, but it didn't really matter. Although I'd

186

be wearing my bathing trunks, I didn't want to get my face and upper body sunburned. In fact, the entire Mediterranean had looked so flat and calm I thought I could even wear my straw hat while swimming. The best plan, however, would be to lay claim to one of those palm-frond umbrellas and hang out in its shade with a root beer float and, hopefully, binoculars.

I think we were all turning into Spaniards because, after dinner, it was closing in on midnight by the time Liza and the girls and I were really into flinging ourselves around on a dance floor to the driving beat of a salsa band in one of the omnipresent tapas bars.

Another good thing: my dancing must have improved considerably because always before when Liza and I had danced the watching girls had laughed.

Now when they laughed, I didn't think they were laughing at me. In order to keep up with the girls, I'd spent as much time as possible watching the real Spanish dancers. Now I thought I was stomping around and wiggling my hips as well as the other guys, because, while I couldn't hear what the watching girls were saying, I was pretty sure it was all flattering.

But for some reason Liza had trouble loosening up. Usually when we danced, she was the dervish and I was as wooden as Pinocchio. But that evening, on the dance floor with me, she tended to dance like a little kid in her first cotillion who was afraid of making a mistake in front of her mother.

At first she had suffered the girls' jibs in frigid silence, but gradually she thawed until now she, too, frolicked around the dance floor like a professional.

By 1:00 o'clock in the morning I was having so much fun I'd forgotten all about paparazzi or even

187

golden girls.

But some part of my mind would not give up, and when I did get to sleep long after midnight my mind spent the rest of the night tormenting me with vivid pictures of Simon and Bruno taking pictures in the nude. Not me. Them. A really horrible nightmare.

CHAPTER 20

Early the next morning, at about 11:00 o'clock, Liza, somehow, was able to herd her brood to the outdoor tables for breakfast.

I could have used a few more hours of sleep. After all the dancing last night, and my wild dreams, my body felt like it would have been able to star in one of those zombie movies.

But it really was a lovely day, even though the brilliant sun attacked my eyes with zillions of photons, each one like a tiny barbed arrow. In the warm sunlight, the cerulean Mediterranean lolled languidly. Liza had told everyone that when the shops closed for siesta, we could spend that time on the beach.

I was a little disappointed that when we did hit the sand, the ladies were wearing bikinis and thigh-length robes they left open in front enticingly. They looked so lovely that my eyes, though weary, would not so much as blink. Even Liza wore a bikini that revealed a figure so enchanting I couldn't believe I had been unaware of its devastating...uh...charms until now.

I noticed I'd been right about spiky-haired Dawn having tattoos. Nestled in the small of her back was the small figure of a unicorn. That was it as far as I could see, and her bikini didn't hide much. I wondered if the daughter of a billionaire would have a tattoo. Possibly. Today it seemed that everybody had a tattoo somewhere. Some people---probably with self-esteem problems---were walking billboards.

But enough speculation. I was ready for a day of relaxation, a day of loafing in the famous Costa Dorada sunlight. I'd augmented my knee-length, camouflage-

189

patterned trunks with a Banana Republic T-shirt and my new wide-brimmed straw hat. I thought I looked fashionably Malibu, although I didn't catch any of the ladies sneaking admiring looks at me.

As usual they were laughing about their night life adventures, not in the least concerned about how many hearts they had broken nor how many married men they had caused to have dreams accompanied by blissful sounds they had to explain to their wives.

Now, after the stony-faced waiters had cleared the table, Liza led the way to one of the palm-frond umbrellas and gave each girl a beach blanket to spread over the warm sand.

She also had a blanket for herself but none for me, and I asked her about that. Her eyes were so stony when she stared at my shorts and T-shirt I thought they would start shooting out some kind of death ray. "You don't need a blanket," she said. "You're wearing one."

My scathing reply was preempted by Valerie pointing to several small white-painted cubicles situated near the hotel at the edge of the beach and asking, "What are those?"

"Oh, I know," Dawn answered. "They're for changing clothes. We have them at Lake Havasu."

"I know, I know," Maria said. "I saw them in a movie. Rita Hayworth, I think."

"Who's Rita Hayworth?" Heather asked.

Dawn gestured languidly. "One of those James Bond girls. A really old one, when movies were all black and white. Isn't that right, Liza?"

"I really couldn't say," Liza answered. "I've never seen a James Bond movie."

The four girls looked at her as though she had

190

told them she was from Mars. "No James Bond?" Dawn said. "What do you look at?"

Before Liza could answer Valerie said, "I know, I know. Those Brad Pitt movies. Right?"

"Right," Liza said. Although I had a feeling she was lying. It wouldn't have surprised me if she'd said she didn't look at any movies unless they were documentaries about saving kids in Africa.

Heather changed the subject by looking around as she said, "Where are all the people? I thought this was supposed to be a famous beach."

Now that she pointed it out, I noticed we seemed to be pretty much alone. There were a few people farther down the beach, even a few with children, but none in front of the hotel.

"That's right, Liza," Maria said. "You said we were going to see a nude beach, but nobody's here."

"Where are the boys?" Dawn said. "There's supposed to be nude gigolos."

"Yes, Liza," Valerie said. "You promised. Remember?"

Liza stood up and looked around with her hand over her mouth while she thought about it as the other girls complained, "That's right, Liza. A nude beach. It was in the brochure."

Slowly, Liza's gaze traversed the nearly deserted beach until they came to me, where they stopped. Uh, oh. There was that look again. I immediately tried to think of a way to bury myself in the sand, or at least, to find a tree to climb. But I didn't have a shovel and palm trees were full of thorns. All I had were my feet.

I leaped up. "I'm going for a swim," I said, and headed for the blessed water, with any luck, I could easily drown.

Too late. Liza already had my arm in an iron grip. "Come," she said. "We've got to talk."

I shook my head. "No, we don't. No talking." I tried to pull away from her grasp. "Swimming. Time for a swim. A long swim. Way out."

She only tightened her grip. "Come with me."

She began dragging me away. I was stronger than she was and could probably have wrestled free, but it would not only have meant giving up my life to the cruel sea, but also **giving up my** summer job.

So I allowed her to drag me away. I would just have to rely on my superior wits to talk my way out of whatever evil thing she had in mind.

She stopped near one of the small white changing booths. "They booked us in the wrong hotel."

"The wrong hotel. This one is nice."

"But this isn't a nude beach. It's supposed to have a nude beach."

I began to breathe again. "Right. The wrong hotel. No nude beach."

"There has to be. It's in the contract."

That darn contract. I had to tear it... Wait! This might not be all bad. "I'll tell the girls," I said. "They can get nude in these little houses."

Liza blinked. "The girls?"

"Right. Right. You can start. You promised. Remember. It's in the contract."

She had to have a mind that worked faster than the speed of light. "Not us," she snapped. "You."

My own mind was racing like an out of control NASCAR. Unfortunately, it was racing around an oval track. In a nano second I was right back where I'd started.

192

"Me? Oh, no. I can't. Not in front of people. I don't even have a mirror in my bedroom."

"There's nobody else. You can do it."

"There is. There is. You. The girls. The waiters."

"You've got to. It's in your contract."

"No, it isn't. I'd remember. The word 'nude' is not in the contract. No where. No way."

"Exactly."

"Exactly?" I didn't like the sound of that. "What does that mean?"

"Your contract does not mention nudity. Therefore, it's not an exception. Go take off your clothes."

I sucked in precious air. "I can't. I can't. I don't even sleep in the nude. I wear a towel when I shave. I don't even have any baby pictures."

"Doesn't matter." She turned me toward one of the white cubicles and gave a shove. "Go. I'll wait here."

I didn't rush to the cubicle. It was only a few steps away, but I tried to make the journey last while I sorted through my options. But other than actually quitting, I couldn't think of a single one.

I was still thinking when I ran out of time. I went inside the small cubicle and heard the door slam behind me. Liza. She wasn't taking any chances.

How long does it take to strip off a T-shirt and climb out of baggy swim trunks? I figured about an hour would be about right. By then the ladies would get tired of waiting and go home.

Liza must have read my mind because she pounded on the door. "Time's up," she said. "Get out here. Now!"

193

Oh, Lordy, Lordy. Frantically, I searched for a savior. And I found one! My hat! Hats don't count as clothes.

Instead of wearing my big straw hat, I held it strategically in front of my nude body. Low in front. I shoved the door open and, smiling broadly, stepped out.

The plan worked perfectly, except for one thing. I'd forgotten to consider what would happen when I was naked in the presence of sexy females. Liza stood before me in her tiny bikini, her face set in a rigor of shock, sunlight highlighting her splendid body making her look like a Playboy centerfold: long legs, gorgeous hair, magnificent shoulders, amazing.... And it happened. Oh, Lordy! Lordy!

"No, no," she said. "No hat. Drop the hat."

I shook my head, clutching the hat with both hands. "No."

"It's in the contract," She stared at the hat. "Let go of the hat."

Something came over me, a kind of devil-may-care impulse that told me to make her pay for her truculence.

I couldn't help myself. I said, "Okay," and LET GO OF THE HAT!

But, of course, THE HAT DIDN'T FALL.

Liza's eyes widened. Then the reason why the hat didn't fall hit her, and in a split second her face turned from white to a full bloom of red. She gasped, "Oh, my God." And she ran.

"Come back," I called. "It's in the contract!"

Naturally, she didn't stop.

I went back in the changing booth and gently closed the door so no one would hear my triumphant

194

laugh.

CHAPTER 21

Liza didn't reappear until late in the afternoon so I'd been stuck with the mind-boggling task of chaperoning the four girls in their bikinis---after I'd put on my own baggy shorts and shirt, of course. Would you believe, I was getting paid for lying around in the sunshine pretending not to stare at four gorgeous girls. Truthfully, it was a job I would have taken for free.

My macho image must have improved considerably with the girls because they pretty much spent the entire afternoon laughing at Liza and looking around for some really macho nude men. But none ever showed up, nor any nude females either. The few women I did see wore bathing suits but would have looked better fully clothed.

Not once did the girls make so much as a move toward the water. But I went for a couple of swims, after making sure the paparazzi goons were nowhere around. I didn't really expect they would be. Pepe said they'd been pretty banged up by the bulls. They might have been calf bulls, but they were big calves with half-grown horns they knew how to use. So, Simon and Bruno would probably be out of action for some time.

When Liza finally did return she was fully dressed. She had apparently regained her composure because she looked at her watch and in her managerial voice said, "It will soon be time for dinner. Why don't you ladies get changed."

She didn't bother telling me to change clothes for dinner. Either she was still miffed at me or didn't want me along.

But I wasn't going to be left out. Buying my own

dinner was not in my contract. That was one thing I was sure of.

Knowing pretty much how long it was going to take the ladies to get dressed for dinner, I took my time getting ready. I'd taken a shower and was shaving when there was a knock on my door.

Liza? I'd been wondering when she'd show up to give me a dressing down for being a smart-ass. I'd been thinking about my defenses, however, and I was ready for her berating. The fact that we were on the wrong beach could hardly be considered my fault. I believe I would have been entirely within my rights to have refused to cooperate. Even so, I had manned-up and followed orders. Again, it wasn't my fault that being naked in the presence of gorgeous girls in bikinis had produced a result she should have anticipated. After all, when one is a macho male such primordial instincts are definitely out of one's control. It's in the genes. Not my fault. Not my fault at all. That should have been in the contract. So sue me.

Now I was only wearing a towel tied around my waist and I didn't want the same thing to happen if the person at the door proved to be one of the girls, and I headed for the closet with the idea of throwing on pants and shirt before I let her in. I stopped. Only a towel? It might be Liza. Seeing me wearing only a towel would surely drive her away.

I opened the door.

It wasn't Liza. It was Heather!

She stood smiling still wearing her bikini and robe, but now augmented with high-heeled pumps which made her seem to be about seven feet tall.

"Heather," I gasped. "What is it? What's wrong?"

197

"Not me," she said. "You. Sunburn" She held up a bottle. "Baby Oil This'll help."

She walked past me, closing the door behind her.

I stood, transfixed, clutching my towel with both hands. "Sunburn?"

"Look at you. All over. I thought so."

I glanced down at my chest. "No, no. No sunburn. Tan. I've got a great tan." I started to lift my arms and turn so she could see I had no sunburn, but even though the towel was tied around my waist, letting go of it did not seem like a good idea.

"This will help." She unscrewed the cap from the bottle. "Lie down on the bed."

Frantically, I searched for escape, expecting either Liza or the police to break down the door any second. Of the two, I hoped it would be the police.

"No," I said. "No sunburn. I have to dress for dinner. You have to dress...for dinner or something."

"Dinner won't be for hours. Lie down."

Hours? With a beautiful Viking rubbing oil on my almost-nude body. My brain began a life-or-death battle with my glands. Why not? It would probably even be worth the twenty years I would spend in a Spanish jail. On the other hand, I would be an old man when they let me go and I wouldn't have such problems.

"Tomorrow," I whispered. "Tomorrow would be better."

"No. Now." She pushed me. My wobbly legs gave up a fight they wanted to lose, and I fell face down across the bed. I felt the bed shake as Heather climbed on and knelt beside me. Oh, Lordy, Lordy.

Some survival instinct inside made me grab the

198

bed sheet and pull it over my body. Heather yanked it off. "Turn over," she said. "We'll start with your chest."

Turn over? The thought of twenty years in jail abruptly escalated to thirty. "My back." I buried my face in the bedding. "It's really bad."

My voice was muffled, but she understood. "Okay," she said. "We've got lots of time. Let's get this towel off."

She grabbed my towel. I grabbed my towel. She tugged. I fought. Well, I did. I really did. But Lordy. She was really, really strong.

I was definitely losing the towel when there was another knock on the door. Startled, Heather let go of the towel.

"Who's that?" she said. "Were you expecting someone? Dawn? I might have known she---"

"No, no," Keeping my voice to a hoarse whisper, I said, "The police. It's probably the police."

"Police." She almost leaped off the bed. "Are you a minor?"

"Yes," I said quickly, grasping at the straw she'd thrown me. "Fifteen. I'm only fifteen. Maybe twelve, thirteen."

The knock sounded again and Liza's voice called, "Calvin. I've got to talk to you."

Liza? Oh, No! I sprang off the bed and practically dragged Heather to the closet. "It's Liza," I said. and flung open the closet door. "Quick. In here!"

Taking the bottle of oil from her hand, I shoved her into the closet. Her eyes were wide with shock as I said, "Don't make a sound," and closed the door.

Hiking up my towel, I called to Liza. "Hold on. I'm coming." On the way to the door I grabbed a T-shirt and slipped it on.

199

With a hurried silent prayer that Heather would not make a sound that would get me killed, I opened the door. Dressed as she had been when I'd last seen her, Liza stared at me, her face grim. Did she know about Heather? Did she even suspect?

"Liza," I said. My heart was pounding, but I managed to keep my voice remarkably calm. "What is it?"

She walked in. I checked the hallway for signs of police before I started to close the door. I hesitated. Better to leave it open. Maybe she would go away.

"Close the door," she said. "We've got to talk. It's important."

When had she ever talked to me that wasn't important? I closed the door. "I was just going to take a shower. We can talk at dinner."

"This can't wait."

I moved so I was standing between her and the closet. "I'm not going to do that nude thing again," I said. "Once was enough."

"You won't have to. Tomorrow we go to Barcelona. This is something else."

Well, that was good news. I edged toward the bathroom. "Give me a minute to put on some clothes."

She saw the bottle of oil I'd left on the dresser and picked it up. Oh, oh. "Baby oil" she said. "Did you get sunburned?"

"Uh...yeah, yeah. A little."

"Take off your shirt. I'll put some on your back?"

Well, this was a strange turn of events. Liza? Putting oil on my back? Did I want that? Oh, yeah.

But I heard my idiot voice say, "No, no. It isn't that bad."

200

"I'm sorry about what happened," she said. "But we really had no choice."

"I understand. It's in the contract."

"That's right. In the contract."

"But if there ever is a next time,"—I gave her my evil smile—"you have to join me."

"It's a deal."

Huh? I'd expected her to throw the bottle at me. Like a complete dolt, I said, "It is? Maybe we should stay here another day."

But being female, her mind was already on other things. "You've got baby oil on your shirt. I'll get you another."

She started toward the closet, and I quickly moved to head her off. "No, no. It's okay." I tried to think of something that would get her body and her mind moving in a new direction. "You said it's important. What is it?"

It worked. She put the bottle of baby oil on the dresser. "It is. I'm really worried."

She made a move toward a chair as though she wanted to stay and talk. But no telling how long Heather would stay quietly in the closet. Also if whatever Liza was going to say might effect our tour, I was pretty sure she wouldn't want one of the girls to hear.

I took hold of her arm and kind of edged her toward the door. "Not here," I said. "The walls are pretty thin. Somebody might hear. Let's go outside."

"Well, all right."

Keeping hold of her arm, I opened the door and practically pushed her out.

She started to turn back. "Wait. Don't you want to get dressed?"

201

I hesitated for about half a second. If I went into the bathroom where I could be alone to put on my pants, Heather might make some kind of sound that would cause Liza to check the closet. I couldn't take the chance.

I pulled the door shut. "The beach. There's going to be a full moon. We can walk on the beach."

She gave me a peculiar glance before she said, "That might be nice."

I **began walking** her down the hall. "**Right. Walk** in the moonlight. Build up an appetite."

She stopped. "Aren't you going to lock your door?"

Lock V Heather inside? Again I hesitated. It might be nice to have her waiting when I came back from walking in the moonlight. But my sense of self-preservation won out. "This is Spain," I said. "Locking the door would be an insult."

"Not for a girl."

"Good point."

I was already leading us away, and she didn't protest. There was a side door guests could use to enter or leave the hotel so they wouldn't have to cross the lobby, probably to keep them from tracking sand inside, and we used it to walk out onto the beach.

The sun had finally gone down, leaving a gentle glooming and a deserted beach. The sand, still warm from the afternoon sun, felt good on my bare feet. When I began to lead the way toward the water, Liza stopped.

"Wait," she said. Removing a ribbon, she shook her hair free so it swirled around her face and shoulders. I guess I stared, totally surprised at what a change it made in her features. With the waves of

202

lustrous hair framing her face, all her stern demeanor vanished, whisked away by an enchanting tangle, leaving her face a soft, beguiling beauty. Then she slipped off her shoes and smiled. "Ready?"

I had to shake myself free of a paralyzing shock before I could move. "You should wear your hair like that all the time."

"I would but...it sometimes gets in the way."

"It isn't that long."

"I don't mean that way. I mean the image."

"What image?"

She began walking slowly and I fell in close beside her. She didn't answer right away, and we walked in silence, our feet in the warm sand, a rising full moon beginning to spread a path of silver on the still Mediterranean water. It had been a long time since I had felt so...content

"My job," she said. "I've got to maintain an image with the ladies. I want to be friends, but I've still got to maintain some distance. I can't really be one of them."

"Like walking a tightrope."

"Sort of."

"Well, you've been doing great so far. Everything under control."

"Thanks. But..."

She didn't finish her sentence so I prompted her: "Something wrong?"

"I don't know and that's what bothers me."

"That's why you came to see me?"

"Yes."

A tingle of alarm made me hesitate before I said, "Is it me? Have I done something?" And like a fool I added, "It isn't my fault. I had no idea she'd do such a

203

thing."

She stopped walking. "She? What are you talking about?"

Oh, oh. How could I dig my way out of my blunder. "Not she, so much. Them. The girls. Staying up half the night. I'm starting to run down."

She made a soft chuckle. "You? You're right out there on the dance floor, too, cutting up a storm."

"You, too," I countered. "Talk about image."

Then she did laugh, until some thought cut off the laugh. "That isn't the problem."

By this time we were walking in the damp sand near the water where the only sounds where the gentle lap of the sea rippling on the shore and the distant sounds of automobiles in the city.

The trace of doubt in her voice made me desperate to help. "There's a problem?" I said.

"It's those men. That's why I came to see you."

The paparazzi? I hastily said, "I had nothing to do with them. I'm innocent."

"I don't mean that," she said, and I relaxed a smidgen. "I just don't understand why they're bugging us. Why us? Do you have any ideas?"

Did I have ideas? I'll say. But I couldn't tell her, so I shook my head. "Not really. I just thought they kind of saw an opportunity to get some pictures of pretty American girls in Spain. There's probably a big market for them."

"That's what I thought, too, but I'm not so sure."

"Oh, why not?"

"Their persistence for one thing. You'd think they'd give up by this time. I keep wondering if it's something more."

204

I didn't like the way this conversation was heading, but I did want to find out how much she knew about one of the girls being a potential gold mine.

"Something more?" I asked.

"Well, maybe they're criminals of some kind. Maybe trying to rob us or—"

She stopped and I finished the thought for her, "---kidnap the girls?"

"Well, yes."

I walked a few steps while I tried to think of a way to sidetrack her idea. The problem was that she was probably right. But for the wrong reason. Since she didn't know that one of the girls came from a particularly wealthy family, she probably thought the goons were after the girls for some more nefarious reason, and what other reason could there be: selling them to some rich Asian or Middle Easterner or, perhaps, the goons would keep them for themselves. That made more sense, judging how homely they were. They probably couldn't get a girl the regular way.

But whatever their reason, the result would be the same: we had to stop them. Hopefully, their bout with the bulls had discouraged them to the point of quitting.

"I don't think you need to worry about them anymore," I said. "Time in the hospital should make them change their minds."

"I hope so."

She took hold of my arm and her shoulder brushed mine. I shivered, a little chill of pleasure.

She glanced at me, "Cold?"

I started to say something clever, but it occurred to me that this was the opening I needed to get some information. "No," I said. "Just a thought, about...us."

I could almost hear her eyebrows shoot up. "Us? You and me?"

"I mean, the future. When this is over. Are you going to stay with Kimberly?"

"I suppose so. This is my first real chance to manage a tour. So far—believe it or not—I'm having a good time, except for those paparazzi."

"Me, too," I said. No point in telling her that filling in for bull fighters and flamenco dancers was not my idea of a good time, but thus far I had not only survived I had triumphed. And, after all, being on tour with four gorgeous girls wasn't bad, five counting Liza. NOW counting Liza.

I walked a little closer to her, our hips practically touching. This tour was shaping up. From now on it would really be fun....or I should say 'could' be fun.

Then I remembered Heather in my closet. If Liza ever found out, the fun could end abruptly and probably my life, too.

By the time we finally headed back to the hotel, I was on pins and needles thinking she might want to see me to my room where Heather might be waiting in the middle of my bed.

But at the hotel Liza headed for her own room, and I walked her to her door where she unlocked and opened it. I expected her to say good night and quickly go in. Instead, she kind of hesitated, then turned to face me. "I enjoyed the walk," she said. "Thanks."

"So did I."

For about two seconds I thought about kissing her good night, then she said, "We'll meet for dinner in about an hour. Barcelona tomorrow. Better read up on those travel brochures."

206

She went in and closed the door. Any romantic hopes I had vanished when I heard the door lock click.

When I got back to my room, Heather was gone.

Instead of being disappointed, I actually felt vastly relieved, rightfully concluding that now I would be allowed to live another day. But I did wonder what she had been going to tell me. Could she have been ready to confess that she was the golden princess? Or maybe she wasn't going to tell me anything, and had simply been attracted to me? I wanted to believe it was the former, but some part of my ego---obviously, the part with a death wish---wanted it to be the latter. I should be so lucky.

After dinner it turned into another wild night of tapas, music and dance. Or I should say a 'mini' wild night. The town was relatively small and there weren't as many disco joints and tapas bars as there were in the big cities.

Fortunately, the few there were weren't that crowded. I wondered why until it dawned on me that most of the tourists in town were not Spanish, and unlike the natives, weren't used to staying up until 3:00 or 4:00 o'clock in the morning. The girls and I, on the other hand, had practically turned into natives. The transition for the girls, seemingly, had been easy, but my body still protested at the late hours. Since, apparently, there was no longer any danger from paparazzi, I resolved to desert the ladies tonight, go back to my room, do my studying, and hit the sack early.

It didn't quite work out that way. Did I say 'quite?' I wasn't even close.

Maybe I shouldn't have changed into my 'going-out-in-the-evening' jeans and a black, long-sleeved shirt. It seemed a shame to waste all that effort on a quick dinner, gorging on a few tapas and dancing for only a few minutes with five wild, beautiful women. Stupid me. As usual, none of us got back to our rooms before 3:00 o'clock in the morning.

CHAPTER 22

I paid the price the next morning when I had to force myself out of bed at the break of 11:00 A.M.

After brunch Pepe drove us up the coast to Barcelona where we were scheduled to spend two days.

The short distance between our beach and Barcelona didn't give the girls time to catch up on their sleep during the drive, so after we checked into the hotel everyone sacked out in siesta naps.

I had just managed to drift into a well-earned nap---which took me about twenty seconds---when the hotel phone rang. I debated on whether to answer it. If it were Liza with another of her emergencies, one that might put me in a hospital or a jail, I didn't want to answer.

On the other hand, if it were one of the girls, perhaps the golden girl herself, I definitely wanted to talk to her.

So, putting myself in the hands of lady luck, I answered the call.

"Calvin?" A man's voice, speaking my name inquiringly, a vaguely familiar man's voice. Well, that was a surprise.

Still I was cautious when I replied with a simple, "Yes?"

"How's the tour going?"

I knew that voice. I'd heard it before, but I couldn't place it. Maybe it was due to distortion caused by the phone so I was cautious when I answered, "Okay. Who is this?"

There was a brief pause as thought the man couldn't believe I didn't recognize him immediately.

"It's me, Charles. Charles Kimberly."

Oh Lordy, Lordy. The boss. And I hadn't recognized his voice. Thinking fast, I said, "I thought it was you, but these phones over here. I can hardly hear you."

His shouted reply almost broke my eardrum. "I said how's the tour going?"

"Oh, I can hear you now. Great. No *problemas*. That's Spanish."

"**Good. But how is that other...uh...** consideration going?"

"Consideration," I racked my mind to think what he meant, and my superior intellect leaped to the rescue. The golden girl.

"Oh, that," I said. "Well, not so—"

He interrupted me. "Hold on. We'd better not discuss this on the phone."

Not discuss it on the phone? I tried to think of alternatives: E-mail? Twitter? Telegrams? They would be even more insecure. Maybe he wanted me to fly back home for a face-to-face conference. But by the time I got there the tour would practically be over and the girls would also be heading home. So I said, "Uh...what did you have in mind?"

"I'm here," he said. "Come to see me."

"Here? In Spain?" I hoped my voice didn't sound as surprised as I felt. What the devil was he doing in Spain? Checking up on me? Was I in some kind of trouble? Had he heard about the episode at the nude beach? Who would have told him? Liza, of course. Darn!

"In Barcelona, actually."

"Oh. Are you coming to the hotel?" He would know, of course, where we were staying.

210

"No, no. I want to keep this confidential. Between us. You come here."

"Uh, okay. Where are you staying?"

"Not far. Actually, I'm on a yacht. Do you know where the Port Olympic marina is?"

Was I supposed to know that? After all, I was the tour guide. I guess he expected me to know everything, so I made a wild guess, "Near the ocean? I mean the sea. The Mediterranean."

There was brief pause while he digested my erudite answer, "True," he said. "Take a taxi. They'll know. When you get here take Muella Gregal. That's a street. At the end turn on Carres de Xaloc. We're at the end near the boat repair place. Look for a hundred-thirty foot motor yacht named 'Ulysses'" He paused as though asking someone a question, which gave me a chance to cut in.

"Hold on a minute," I said. "I want to write those down."

I dug a pen and a piece of paper out of a drawer and he spelled the names for me, ending with, "Berth two. Near the boat repair place."

A hundred-thirty-foot yacht in berth two? That spelled money, big money. "Got it," I said. "I'm leaving now."

Since I had no idea how far away this Port Olympic was from our hotel, which was near the center of the city, I didn't want to set a time for my arrival.

"Okay," he said. "Shouldn't take long. We'll be waiting."

"Oh, wait," I quickly said before he could hang up. "Do you want me to bring Liza?"

"No, no. I told you: she's not in on this. Come alone."

211

"Uh, okay. Roger that."

"Make it fast." He hung up.

I stood for a moment staring at the phone in my hand as though it could answer the questions swirling through my mind. What was Mr. Kimberly doing in Spain? Was it solely because of our tour group, or was he on some kind of vacation and the two of us being in Barcelona was purely a coincidence? I snorted in disgust and hung up the phone. I would have to be a total idiot to believe it was coincidental.

He said that Port Olympic marina was not far away. I would soon find out the truth. I was sure of only one thing: the truth would not be good. Not for Calvin Dorsey.

CHAPTER 23

I dressed in a hurry while trying to ignore the kaleidoscopic thoughts that continued to swirl though my mind. No matter from which direction I approached it, this meeting could not produce good news. Had Mr. Kimberly come all the way to Spain just to check up on me? I know I had been derelict in calling him. More likely, it was because of this elusive golden girl. Obviously, he still didn't know who she was and, by this time, assumed that I would have found out. Why did he even want to know? As long as Kimberly Tours was getting their fee and things were going well, there was no reason for him to know.

On the other hand, if I owned the travel agency and, therefore, was responsible for such a person, I doubt that I would sleep well until the tour was over and she had been safely returned to her parents---whoever they were.

What would he say when I told him I had no more idea who she was than when we'd started? I doubted he would be pleased.

After hurriedly dressing I started to call the hotel's concierge to get a taxi when it occurred to me that I had little money to pay for a taxi. Maybe I could take a bus. They shouldn't cost much. And if Mr. Kimberly fired me, he would have to pay me for my time up to now. I had my plane ticket to return home. Still, money could be a problem.

Then, as usual, I thought of a solution: Pepe. He would surely know where this Port Olympic marina was located. And if Mr. Kimberly fired me because I'd allowed Pepe to drive me to the place, Pepe could get

213

me back to the hotel for my luggage, then to the airport.

Wait a minute. Mr. Kimberly didn't have to know. If Pepe waited out of sight, Mr. Kimberly would assume I'd come by taxi as he'd suggested. Problem solved.

I called Pepe on his cell phone, and when he answered, I asked if he could take me to this 'Port Olympic marina.' He said he knew where it was and would meet me in the hotel lobby.

As we were driving I apologized for breaking up his siesta, and I rather expected him to ask why I wanted to go alone to this port in the middle of the afternoon. But he didn't ask, much to my relief, because I didn't really have a good answer. He seemed his usual jovial self and didn't ask me to explain.

It proved to be a short drive. Our hotel was situated near an old part of town that I think is called Ciutat Villa. Anyway, it's fairly near the waterfront, and it turned out that this Port Olympic Marina was on the north-east end of the port area. On the way Pepe even pointed out a few restaurants that were famous for their seafood.

Near a towering building that Pepe said was the famous Hotel Arts, we turned toward the water on our right, and after only a short distance, arrived at what Pepe said was Port Olympics Marina.

I exclaimed, "Holy smoke." I'd expected a small kind of harbor with a few boats, but what I saw made me stare. It really was a marina, a huge square-shaped, man-made port about the size of four football fields, containing about a thousand boats. Most were sail boats, but many were motor boats. I didn't know how large a boat had to be to qualify as a yacht, but I was sure a lot of them would make the grade.

Pepe said the port had been constructed for the 1969 Olympics and had been converted into a yacht harbor.

As well as I could in my pigeon Spanish, I told him the street names I'd written down. He looked blank until I mentioned the boat repair place. He knew it was at the end of a long, land-fill wharf and went right to it.

There was a huge parking area on the wharf that was almost deserted so Pepe was able to park near the end. Several good-sized yachts were berthed nearby, but it wasn't difficult to pick out a big white one with the name 'Ulysses'. In Idaho and Arizona we don't see many yachts, but I'd read enough to know that this one had to be in the megayacht class. I didn't see any sails so I assumed it wasn't a sailing yacht. What had Mr. Kimberly called it: a 'motor' yacht. It had two decks and a long bow in front of the main cabin holding what could have been a really small swimming pool. More likely it was a Jacuzzi. A Jacuzzi on the deck? Wow! I was impressed.

Telling Pepe to wait for me, I walked to a little gangway that lead to the yacht's back end and called, "Hello, the Ulysses."

Mr. Kimberly immediately came out of the cabin.

"Calvin," he said."

I'd kind of expected him to be wearing some kind of all-white yachting clothes with white sneakers and one of those neat navel officer's caps, but he was wearing his usual grey pants and a blue jacket over a white shirt.

I started to walk aboard, then stopped when I

215

remembered something I'd read. I grinned and said, "Am I supposed to ask 'permission to come aboard'?"

He laughed. That was good. "No," he said. "Come on aboard."

I sauntered onboard, and he held out his hand. "Good to see you."

I didn't really believe him. I was pretty sure he hadn't come all the way from Phoenix just to shake my hand, but I replied, "You too."

I took a quick look around the boat. Everything looked new: the paint was pure white with no scuff marks; all the visible wood was highly polished, looking expensive. Every bit of metal appeared to be made of gleaming copper. I would have bet the whole thing cost more than a few thousand dollars. "I didn't know you had a yacht," I said.

"Oh, it's not mine," he said. "Come on. I'll introduce you to..."---he hesitated---"the owner."

I followed him through a doorway into a good-sized cabin that smelled of rich leather. I could see why. The room was about twenty-five feet long and at least fifteen feed wide and furnished like a really expensive drawing room with benches along the sides all upholstered in white leather. In the middle of the room, gleamed like a mirror, was a long directors-table, that could have been made of teak wood. Big comfortable-looking chairs around it were upholstered in—what else—white leather. The floor was covered with a thick white carpet. I wondered how they kept it dry when the boat was being flung around in a storm. There had to be a way to seal the room off so no water got in. I wondered what it would be like to be enjoying the Jacuzzi in the bow during a storm. That would be really cool, if you didn't get sea sick.

216

A door up front opened and a short, thick guy came in. He looked to be in his fifties with thinning hair turning grey and a really healthy tan. This guy really was wearing white pants and shirt and white shoes. Although he didn't have a white captain's cap, he had to be the owner.

He said, "You must be Calvin," and shook my hands with a grip so strong I thought I might be wrong about him being the owner. More likely he was the guy who polished all that copper.

"Calvin," Mr. Kimberly said. "This is...uh... Alfred."

"Pleased to meet you, Mister Alfred," I said. "Or should I call you Captain Alfred?"

He smiled, showing teeth that looked unnaturally white in his deep tan. "Not hardly," he said. "I wouldn't know a port from a starboard. I have a real captain for that."

I noticed his words had an almost imperceptible trace of an accent, but not enough for me to guess his nationality. He indicated one of the chairs. "Sit down, please."

"Thanks," I said as it sat down in one of the white chairs facing the table. "I'm not sure what the rules are onboard a ship."

"No rules allowed," he said. "That's why I have my own yacht."

That made sense. I knew that when a ship is at sea the captain is God. I'd bet that even though Alfred had a captain to handle the boat, when they were at sea---or in port---he was still God.

He and Mr. Kimberly took seats at the table. Mr. Kimberly said, "Mister ...uh...Alfred and I have been friends for...uh...quite some time."

217

They might be old friends, but I noticed he'd called him 'Mister' Alfred.

"What can I get you to drink?" Mr. Alfred said. I kind of glanced around, but I didn't see anything to drink, and I couldn't picture the man leaping up to fetch something from the kitchen, wherever that was.

As though on command, the door opened and a muscular fellow wearing white pants and shoes and a white T-shirt that displayed his muscles came in carrying a tray so loaded with glasses and bottles I don't think I could have lifted it. I noticed the fare included a large champagne bottle nestled in a silver bucket that I assumed was filled with ice. He set the tray on the table near Mr. Alfred and stepped back. Mr. Alfred raised an eyebrow at me. "A glass of wine, or would you prefer champagne? Perhaps a martini?"

I wouldn't have been surprised if he'd asked if I wanted bootleg gin, which was probably somewhere on that tray. But I just said in my deepest, macho baritone, "Perrier. Uh...make that a double."

Mr. Alfred didn't so much as blink, but the bartender guy beside him looked a little nonplussed. He'd probably been expecting me to request a double shot of whiskey. As it was, his hands kind of hovered over the repast before they dived in and, sure enough, lifted out a Perrier bottle.

As the fellow poured me a glass filled to the top, Mr. Alfred asked, "How is the tour going?"

So he knew about the tour. I wondered how much more he knew. Probably everything, or else why would we be here.

"Good," I told him. Not wanting to sound egotistic I added, "Liza is doing a great job. Everything's right on schedule."

"Liza?" He glanced at Mr. Kimberly.

"Our tour manager," he said. "Very competent." He looked at me for confirmation.

"Right. Very competent. Everything copasetic." Mr. Alfred smiled. "Copasetic. I like that."

Mr. Kimberly looked a little puzzled, and I suspected he didn't know what copasetic meant. So I elucidated. "No problems. Things going like clock work. Right on schedule."

"I understand you had a little trouble in the bull ring," Mr. Kimberly said.

Now how did he know that? Probably from Liza. Now that I thought of it, I'm sure she was required to give him daily reports.

It suddenly dawned on me why he had sent for me. It was about those reports. I hadn't been overly punctual. He was probably worried sick that something might have happened to me.

"Uh, sir," I said. "About those daily reports, I know I've been a little lax, but there really—"

He waved his hand, interrupting me. "Tell me about our...uh...guest. What have you learned?"

"Well, sir," I said. "Not much. She's—"

"Do you know which one?"

The way he had brushed aside my attempt to report on the tour made me realize that the only reason he was here was because of the golden princess. He clearly had no interest in anything else. Obviously, he was worried enough to come all the way to Spain to find out. And I had failed him.

"Sorry, sir," I said. "I've been trying to identify her...without her knowing it, of course. That means I've had to go slow. Keep her from becoming suspicious, as it were."

219

It was Mr. Alfred who said, "So, you don't know which one she is."

The kind of demanding way he said it made me glance at Mr. Kimberly, wondering how deep I should go on this subject for the benefit of Mr. Alfred.

He apparently read my mind. "We can discuss this here," he said. "Mr. Alfred is...uh...my partner."

"Oh," I said. "In that case I should tell you, sir, I don't know a thing."

Mr. Alfred leaned forward, his eyes hard, reflecting what I hoped was curiosity. "Not a thing?" he kind of growled. "Are you sure?"

I nodded. I had the clear impression that while Mr. Kimberly might fire me for being a failure, judging by the expression of disbelief on his face, Mr. Alfred would probably have me keelhauled.

"Sorry," I said, and I really was. "I've been watching them ...evaluating them actually... questioning them as much as possible without blowing my cover." I liked that: 'blowing my cover.'

"And you don't have any idea which one she is?" I thought Mr. Alfred had a lot of irk in his voice.

"That's right, sir." I took a swallow of my Perrier just to show that my hands were not shaking. The gesture lost a little of its impact when I had to use both hands.

Mr. Kimberly's hands might not have been shaking, but his voice was definitely making threatening gestures when he said, "How much longer will it take you to find out?"

"I can't be sure," I said. "I think I'm making progress, but..." I made a grimace and my shoulders shrugged.

"If you had to make a guess," Alfred said, "who

220

would it be?"

I looked at Mr. Kimberly. Did he really want me o say anything in front of Mr. Alfred? But I hated to be designated the 'fall guy.' "You know they're pretty much all alike," I said. "You put the package together."

Mr. Kimberly glanced at Mr. Alfred before he said, "Not really." He turned to Mister Alfred. "They came in a package deal, via the telephone and the internet. Sort of fait accompli. I never met the ...uh...agent."

Mr. Alfred started at him a couple of seconds, and I hope he never gave me that look. He wasn't even looking at me and it turned my blood to ice.

Then he did look at me, but with more of a fatherly   'I-won't-kill-you-if-you-don't-lie-to-me' expression. I grinned at him.

He said, "Go ahead. Give it your best shot."

When Mr. Kimberly did not object, I said, "Dawn."

He said, "With that hair? No. The other blonde. Straight hair?"

Heather? What did I know about Heather? About as much as I knew about Dawn. Both of them looked like a million dollars to me. But did I want to tell that to this man? I kind of shook my head. "She's a student. Gorgeous. But strong. I wouldn't want to get in a fight with her."

He kind of grunted before he said, "The redhead."

This was easier. "I doubt it could be her. I never saw any billionaire's picture in Forbes with red hair."

"Could be from her mother."

I tried to think of an objection. I didn't want it to

221

be Valerie. In fact, I didn't want it to be any of them.

"Maria," I said. "My bet is on Maria."

The two men exchanged glances as though I had been caught in a lie. Actually, I'd said Maria because I thought she was the least likely. She looked too much like an exotic Latina model with the energy of a dancer to be the indolent daughter of a billionaire.

But on the other hand....

Mr. Alfred stood up and his lips moved into what could have been a smile. "All right, son. Relax. You've passed the test."

"Test?" My mouth had to be hanging open.

Mr. Alfred nodded to Mr. Kimberly. "Tell him."

Mr. Kimberly also smiled. "His name isn't really Alfred. This isn't really his yacht."

I said noting, too shocked to ask even one of the questions swirling round in my brain.

Finally, I was able to say, "But...why?"

Mr. Alfred's eyes sort of crinkled. "I'm her father," he said.

"Her father?" I couldn't keep the disbelief out of my voice. "The...the billionaire?"

This time he really did smile. "The last time I looked."

"So," I said as the real question spun to the top of my mind. "Which one is she?"

He shook his head. "Better you don't know."

But I had to know. Curiosity was burning a hole in my cool. "But——-"

He lifted his hand, cutting off my question. "You might be able to keep it a secret, but it'll be easier if you don't know." He smiled again. "She'd kill me if anyone found out, even you."

Well, in a way, that made sense. If I found out, I

222

might not be able to hide my desire to marry her. On the other hand... "Will I ever find out?" I asked.

"That's up to her," he said. "If she wants you to know, she'll tell you herself, probably at the end of the tour."

"Okay," I said. "But if I find out, do I get a bonus?"

He gave me a look like my venality really disappointed him. "What did you have in mind?"

"Just kidding," I said hastily.

His smile said he didn't really believe me. "Thank you for coming aboard," he said.

He put his hand out in a friendly gesture, but his eyes accused me of either mendacity or stupidity. I hoped it was the latter. His disappointment had to be because I hadn't been able to identify the golden girl. He obviously thought I had been a poor choice for the job.

His grip on my hand tightened, which I took to be a subtle warning. "Call Kimberly," he said, "if you have any problems."

"Yes, sir," I answered. And I wasn't lying; I really meant it. I'd call him if I were in the middle of an earthquake.

I headed for the door, anxious to leave before Mr. Kimberly actually fired me. He must have understood my trepidation because he escorted me to the door.

When we were out on the stern deck, he said, "Don't tell anyone about this."

"Don't worry," I said. "I won't."

I started toward the gangplank, and he took hold of my arm. "You understand. He's really worried about his daughter."

223

I nodded. "I understand."

"He wants to see her, just to make sure she's okay."

"That shouldn't be a problem. All he has to do is call."

"No," he interrupted. "He doesn't want her to know. If anyone saw them together it would end her anonymity."

He certainly was right about that. Liza might be able to keep the secret, but the other girls would be a bunch of magpies. And they sure wouldn't be able to treat her like one of them after they knew. And me.... Suppose he ask me to bring his daughter to the yacht? Would I be able to treat her like just one of the crowd after I knew? Probably not. I'd be asking her to marry me before we even got back from the visit.

"He doesn't actually have to talk to her," Mr. Kimberly went on. "If we knew where you were going to be tomorrow at, say, five o'clock, we could be watching. He'd see she was okay."

"Oh, good idea," I said, thinking about it. "It would have to be outside. He could be off somewhere, maybe with binoculars."

"Exactly. Where would you suggest? It shouldn't be too crowded."

I didn't want him to know I was a lousy tour guide so I wracked my brain for places I'd read about in Barcelona. The place should be away from crowds, easily observed. Maybe a park. One place popped out.

"The Columbus Monument," I said, trying to remember what it looked like in the pictures I'd seen. "It's in a big open plaza. Not far from here. We could park the SUV far enough away from the monument so he could see us walking to the monument."

He whacked me on the shoulder. "Perfect. Make it as close to five o'clock as you can."

"No problema," I said.

"Good work," he said. "I may even be able to get you that bonus."

He turned back to the cabin, and I was going to walk up the gangway before I remembered to tell him, "Oh, one thing. The paparazzi has been bugging us. Trying to take pictures of the girls."

He turned back. "Two guys? Don't pay any attention to them."

He went into the cabin and closed the door.

Two guys?

I walked to the car with my head down, deep in thought. The paparazzi. It seemed more than a coincidence that they always seemed to know where we would be. Sometimes they even got there ahead of us. Either they had somehow obtain a copy of our itinerary or, more likely, someone was telling them. And how did Mr. Kimberly know it was two guys? Somebody had to have told him. But who? Whom? The same person who was telling the goons where to find us? Not me, that was certain. Liza, no way. One of the girls? That was a possibility, but their knowledge of our route was a little sketchy. Still, It was the most logical explanation.

At least, that's what I thought until I arrived at the place where Pepe was waiting in the SUV, and my acute subconscious added one more name: Pepe. He knew everything. And what did we know about him? Nothing, except that he'd been hired by Kimberly tours. Mr. Kimberly. Maybe Mr. Kimberly had told him that one of the girls was uberwealthy, and he had told those paparazzi. Somebody had, that was certain. And

Pepe was the only one left.

Waiting in the car, he'd been reading a newspaper. When I got in he put it down and raised an eyebrow. "Back to the hotel," I told him.

I knew he had to be curious about my unexpected visit to the yacht, but he didn't ask. Still, I thought it best to give him some kind of explanation, which certainly wouldn't be the truth.

I started to say something when I caught my breath. What the devil? A little yellow car...half hidden in an obscure corner of the marina parking area. The paparazzi? Here?

I had to dismiss the idea. There was no reason for them to be here at Port Olympia. They hadn't followed me from the hotel. Of that, I was certain. Not only that, but: why would they? They sure didn't want pictures of me. Besides, there had to be hundreds of those little yellow cars. It had to be one of them. Pure coincidence.

Still, I considered asking Pepe to go back so I could get another look, but hesitated. If I were wrong, which didn't seem likely, he'd think I was getting paranoid. And if he was the informer, he'd tell them.

I shook my head to clear it of such stupid thoughts. It had to be my bruised and battered imagination.

I set back in the seat, thinking again of concocting a story to tell Pepe about why I had gone to the marina, but I said nothing. It was really none of his business, I hoped.

CHAPTER 24

As usual the Spanish nightlife blew all thoughts of subterfuge from my mind. Pepe directed us to a place called a *multispacios* that featured different rooms for dining, dancing and entertainment. It's hard to think of bad guys when your stomach is full of succulent tapas and your feet are flailing away to the exhilarating beat of Spanish guitars.

But my mind refused to be sidetracked by exotic music and the lithe bodies of lovely girls. Watching the girls dance, motivated my mind more than ever to continue its relentless search for clues that would lead it to the golden girl.

Which one?

Dawn? With her spiky hair, tattoos, brilliant smile? Did she have the brains to sustain such a deception? Plus, it was impossible that the stocky Mr. Alfred could be the father of such long legs and gorgeous body.

But that was also true of Heather. Heather? The athlete with her long, blonde hair, guileless blue eyes and a body that could bend your mind as easily as it could an iron bar. And her mind? Could she pull it off?

Valerie? Who ever heard of a mega-billionaire with red hair so gorgeous it couldn't possibly have come out of a bottle. Her magnificent body might have been crafted in exercise spas, but it obviously had a lovely foundation to begin with. Besides, the abandoned way she danced could not possibly have been influenced by the rigid rules of ballet lessons. And her mind? Who knew?

Maria? Mysterious Maria. Her taciturnism could

be the results of being shut away in an ivory tower during her formative years with only adults for companionship or confidents. Or it could be just a sultry, smoldering sexuality that she kept under control with a unique sense of self preservation. But watching her dance in six-inch heels with her hips sashaying and her hair flying, it was difficult to believe that she could have learned those sexy moves in some ballet class. Still, her physiognomy was closer to that of Mr. Alfred **than any of the other girls. I just had trouble** thinking of her as our golden princess. But maybe that was part of her disguise. I mean, who would think of such an exotic beauty as one of the richest people in the world? Maybe her Latino name was part of the deception. And maybe Mr. Alfred was Middle Eastern, Arabic, for instance, which could mean Saudi oil. Oh, wow. Maria could be an Arabian princess. It worked for me.

The next day, however, in the brilliant sunlight of a Spanish day my deductions tended to change. During brunch the ladies---typically after being rousted out of their beds at the insane time of 10:30 A.M.---did not act like any of them could be blessed with megabucks. They all moved and fraternized as though their lovely bodies and agile minds required a few more hours of sleep to regain even a modicum of the energy they had wantonly dissipated last night.

I thought I could bring them to life by first taking them to the neo-Gothic Temple De La Sagrada Famila, the famous church designed by Antonio Gaudi.

But somehow it did not hold their rapt attention even when I explained how Gaudi himself had overseen construction of the cathedral with its five distinctive spires. I'm not sure they were fascinated

228

when I informed them that Gaudi had died in 1926 as construction was still in progress and the cathedral had never been completed. In fact construction was still going on, which seemed a waste of words since a couple of tall construction cranes flanked the unique spires like modern intruders.

Even a trip to view Gaudi's imaginative architectures of Casa Mila and Casa Batllo had failed to elicit more than a few incongruous remarks about the man who had designed such outlandish structures.

I thought a nice walk along the famous La Rambla with all its beautiful trees, flower beds, art nouveau facades and outdoor restaurants would bring them to life. No matter how much enlightenment about the wide, straight boulevard and how it was laid out and built by the Romans and how, unlike the structures in the South, Barcelona had virtually no Moorish architecture. There was, however, a great deal of evidence---in the form of many red and yellow flags and signs printed in Castilian-Spanish---that the Castilians considered themselves to be separate from the rest of Spain. But no matter how much fascinating information Lisa and I poured into the girls, they still flopped along like zombies.

Stupid me. It wasn't until we moved a block over to the famous shopping district of Passeig de Gracia, that they began to come alive. I should have known by this time that a shop having a sale can bring a female to life much faster than a tour through even the most famous cathedral in the world.

Remembering my promise to Mr. Kimberly to have our group at the Plaza Puerta De La Paz with its regal monument to Columbus by 3:00 P.M., I nudged everyone in that direction by having Pepe drive us

229

through the old Gothic section of Barri Gotic with its narrow streets and ancient stone buildings until he was on the Passaig de Colon heading toward the Columbus Monument plaza.

After we arrived parking places proved to be plentiful in a parking zone in the shade of trees at the edge of the plaza near the Columbus monument. Perfect. If Mr. Alfred was watching from one of the nearby buildings, walking the ladies across the wide plaza to the monument should give him a good view.

But getting the ladies out of the air conditioned SUV into the hot afternoon sun for a walk in the plaza proved to be a chore. With no shopping in sight, they had little interest in a famous 167-foot monument to old Christopher C.

I managed to get them moving by promising that if they would take a look at the monument I would forgo my planned visit to the Royal Palace in favor of a visit to the shops we had missed earlier on the southern end of the nearby Les Rambles.

As we strolled across the plaza toward the base of the monument I tried to figure out where the golden girl's father could be hiding. The best place would be using binoculars from one of the upper floors of the nearby 14th century arsenal building that I had read now housed the maritime museum.

But wherever he was, I tried to give him time for a good look by keeping the girls occupied near the monument while I explained how it had been constructed in 1888 for a Universal Exhibition. Inside the monument was an elevator that went all the way to the top. I was going to suggest we take the elevator ride for a panoramic view of Barcelona until I realized that, once inside the monument, the girl's father would

230

not be able to see her. As it worked out, the ladies weren't wildly enthusiastic about the view anyway.

Walking back to the SUV where Pepe waited went a lot faster than the walk toward the statue, with the girls laughing and joking about shopping, and I hoped that Mr. Alfred—or whatever his name was--- could see that his daughter was healthy and enjoying herself.

It was just as the ladies had all climbed into the SUV and I was getting ready to board that disaster struck.

The little yellow car seemed to come out of nowhere, wheeling into the parking area and screeching to a halt next to the driver's side of our SUV.

Startled, I froze with one foot inside the back door of the SUV when the big paparazzo, Bruno, threw open the passenger door of the yellow car and charged out with astonishing speed for his huge bulk. He yanked open the SUV's front door and grabbed Pepe. To his credit Pepe got in one good punch before Bruno hit him in the head with what looked like a pistol held in his huge paw.

Pepe slumped over the SUV's steering wheel and Bruno dragged him out and dumped him on the ground.

By this time I was charging around the front of the SUV to get at Bruno, and the girls inside were rending the air with shrill screams.

I had started to launch myself at Bruno when he pointed a pistol at me. The gun seemed small in his big hand except that the round hole in end of the gun's barrel looked about the size of an oil drum, and I skidded to a halt. Bruno took one step toward me, and

231

I went into my karate stance, ready to fight to the death, although I had little doubt about whose death it would be.

I was spared the ignominy when Bruno pounded me on the top of he head with his fist holding the gun, and the world spun crazily.

I felt myself slump against the side of the yellow car as I tried to focus my eyes on the blurring image of the yellow car's driver, Simon. He leaped out of the little car and rushed to the SUV where the girls were huddled. By the time they realized they should be out and running, Simon had slid behind the SUV's steering wheel. Bruno was already jammed in the front passenger seat, squeezing Liza between them. If the girls even thought of getting away, they were discouraged by Bruno turning, pointing his pistol at them, and growling, "Don't move!"

Through my blurry vision I saw Lisz claw at Bruno until he whacked her in the side of the head with the gun.

I heard the SUV's motor start, and I just managed to stagger out of its way as it roared in reverse, skidded to a stop, then, its tires squealing, took off out of the parking area.

I tried to run to catch it, and managed about two steps before blacking out. I felt the tarmac of the parking area hitting my left shoulder and the side of my head whacking into the ground.

Strangely, the blow seemed to clear my vision and I tried to get up. But my legs had no strength, and I had to crawl to where Pepe lay sprawled on the ground on his side.

I hesitated about trying to turn him face up, afraid that if he had a back injury any movement might

232

exacerbate it. I checked his carotid artery for a pulse, and the same time croaking, "Pepe. Pepe. Can you hear me?"

To my relief he stirred and tried to lift his head. I was on my knees but feeling stronger, and I helped him sit up. There was a little blood on his temple where Bruno had hit him, but there did not appear to be heavy bleeding. He pressed his fingers on the spot and groaned. I gave him my handkerchief and helped him hold it in place over the wound. He tried to shake his head as though to clear away fog. "Where....where are...they?" he gritted.

Even though my own head was still fighting a lingering darkness, I thought it odd that he had spoken without a trace of an accent.

"Gone," I said. "They got the girls."

"Damn." He pushed to his knees, still holding the handkerchief over his head wound. "I was afraid of that."

"Afraid?" I was having trouble comprehending his words.

He struggled to his feet and took a cell phone from his pocket. Letting go of the handkerchief, he punched in a number. "How long have they been gone?" he asked.

"A couple of minutes."

By this time my head had cleared, and I stared at him. This man was not the Pepe I knew.

He started talking on the phone in a torrent of Spanish. I only caught the word 'policia.'

Fear and anxiety helped me get to my feet. "Who are you?" I said. When he didn't answer, I grabbed his shoulder. "Who the hell are you? Who are those guys?"

He paused for an instant. "Policia," he said. "I don't know who they are."

"I think...," I said. "I think they work for the guy on the yacht."

He held the phone against his chest. "What guy? What did he look like?"

"Stocky, gray hair, about sixty. His name is Alfred. He said he was the girl's father."

He grimaced. "Alfred Parusko. I should have known when I saw the yacht."

"Parusko? Who's he?"

"International criminal."

"And you're a policeman."

"Right."

In a daze, unable to stand, I sat down on the tarmac. They had taken all the girls because they didn't know which one was the right one. And Mr. Kimberly? He had to be working with them.

Pepe started talking on the phone again. I assumed he was putting out an all points bulletin for the SUV.

But they would be too late. If this guy Parusko had planned this, they would be long gone before the police could set up road blocks. But maybe not. Maybe he was not taking the chance of driving around Spain with five screaming women. And it would take them almost an hour to drive to the airport. Plenty of time for the police to set up road blocks and alert airport security. No, he had to have another way to get the girls away. If he intended to take them away. Maybe he'd hole up with them in Barcelona. In the rabbit's wren of houses in the old district alone there had to be hundreds of places to hide.

But five girls? How long could he keep them

234

bottled up? And he would be afraid to kill any of them, afraid he might be killing the goose with the golden eggs.

So the best thing he could do was get the girls away to a place where he could hold them indefinitely, at least long enough to force the golden girl to reveal her true identity, then for the girl's father to come up with a king's ransom.

But how would he do that?

Of course. The yacht.

Mr. Kimberly had said the yacht wasn't his. But what difference did it make who owned it? Parusko had it and once the girls were aboard he could high tail it out of the port, and there were hundreds of places along the Mediterranean coast where he could hide. What was one more yacht among thousands?

I had to stop him. But how?

I grabbed Pepe's arm, "The yacht," I snapped. "They're on the yacht."

He turned to ask me something, but I was already on my feet, running. Several people had gathered to see what had happened, and I pushed past them to the yellow car. I yanked open the driver's door, praying that Simon had been too caught up in the kidnapping to remember the car keys. Sure enough. The key was there in the ignition switch, a chain dangling with a small medallion.

I scrambled in, slammed the door, shoved the gear shift to what I hoped was 'park' and turned the key. The starter ground over and the engine caught. Who said prayer never helped?!

I shoved the gear shift into reverse. If anyone was dumb enough to be behind me when I roared back after a quick glance, he would have been flattened.

But I didn't feel any thumps so I shifted gears into something that got me going forward, and zoomed out of the parking area. I spun onto the Passeig De Colom heading north. I tried to remember the route Pepe had taken to the Port Olympic Marina, but it was useless. Barcelona was a labyrinth of streets; still, I figured that if I stayed as close to the waterfront as possible, eventually I had to reach the Marina.

As I drove, wildly whipping around traffic, totally surprised but immensely grateful for the power in the little car, I tried to struggle into the seatbelt, but had to give it up. If I died, I died.

I had no idea if I was on the correct road, or even going in the right direction, so I was immensely gratified when after about a mile I recognized a towering building ahead of me. The Hotel Arts. This was where Pepe had turned right to get to the Port Olympic marina. So I crossed my fingers and whipped around the first street on my right.

In about a hundred yards, there it was on my left: the marina.

I turned left the way Pepe had done, then cut to the right onto the long parking wharf and headed for the far end. The wharf should end at the boat repair place with the yacht next to it.

Whoa! Our SUV! There it was right where we'd parked yesterday. It was sitting with its doors open, empty. They had to be on board the yacht. And it was berthed right.... Oh, no. Gone. The berth where it had been tied was empty.

Too late. I pounded the steering wheel in frustrated rage.

Wait. How long? How long had they been gone? If Pepe could alert the harbor police---they had to have

236

harbor police---they could intercept it.

Phone? How could I phone the police? I searched for my cell phone. Gone. Lost somewhere.

Phone. I had to find a phone.

But where? The boat repair shop! They had to have a phone.

I jammed the gear into reverse, roared back, made a squealing stop, whipped into gear and raced around the right side of the fenced-in boat repair area, looking for an entrance.

Rounding the back side of the boat repair area, I saw it! Not the entrance: the yacht.

There it was, the big white yacht named 'Ulysses' in the center of the narrow channel, moving slow but picking up speed as it headed for the marina's exit to the open sea.

Oh, Lordy, Lordy.

Once it reached the open sea, it would be out of jurisdiction of the harbor police! I had to stop it! How?

What I needed was a missile of some kind. And I had one. The little yellow car! In the narrow channel, the yacht was only about thirty feet from the wharf. If I could get going fast enough and could time it just right, I could drive off the wharf, sail about thirty feet in the air, and plop down just ahead of the yacht. It would be too late for the big boat to stop. It would run into the yellow car before it could sink, damaging the yacht enough to make it stop. Wouldn't it?

No time to think. Go, go, go.

I jammed the peddle to the medal. The little darling's wheels spun. It leaped forward, sprinting toward the end of the dock, charging toward its doom.

I had no time for finesse, simply trying to change my direction enough to aim for the water ahead of the yacht, but not too far ahead.

Now!

The little car sailed off the side of the pier like an Olympic diver, executed a perfect full twist, and plunged head first into the water, sending up a magnificent geyser--- Oh, no! Not the water of the Mediterranean, the water of the yacht's Jacuzzi!

I scrambled out of the car's open window as the valiant yellow car, its nose buried in a huge hole in the **bottom of the Jacuzzi, was being** sucked down by **the** Jacuzzi's remaining water gushing into the hole like a tree being sucked into a sink hole. Clinging to the deck, I saw the yellow car disappear into the hole and heard it smash into the yacht's hull. I peered down into the hole that used to be the bottom of the Jacuzzi. The little yellow car was dead, standing on its head with its nose crumpled against the yacht's hull. Sea water from huge cracks in the yacht's hull spewed over the car's hot engine, sending a column of steam rising out of the hole like a cloud of doom.

I tried to stagger to my feet, but someone incredibly strong put an arm around my waist and pulled me upright.

Regaining my balance I said, "Thanks."

A deep raspy voice said, "You're welcome."

I half turned so I could see who it was and looked into the brutal face of...Bruno. The other guy, what was his name, Simon, stood behind him.

"Ah ha," I said. "I was right: you're not paparazzi."

Bruno said, "What's a paparazzi?"

I didn't want to waste time explaining. Instead, I said, "You can let go of me now."

For reply Bruno twisted my arms behind my

238

back and clamped my wrists in a big hand.

"Hey," I protested. "You're both under arrest."

"Take him to the cabin," Simon said.

Bruno forced my arms up behind my back so I had to move on tiptoes as he marched me across the deck to the cabin door. Moving ahead of us, Simon opened the door and Bruno, letting go of my hands, shoved me inside the cabin. It took me a couple of steps to retain my balance, and like the snapping of a picture, my agile brain took in the scene. Mr. Kimberly and the gray-haired guy, Alfred Parusko, stood near the big table. The four girls and Liza, sat on the cushioned bench on the side of the room. All of them had their hands behind them as though they were tied and with pieces of duck tape across their mouths.

"Calvin!" Mr. Kimberly said. "What the hell have you done?"

My startled gaze focused on him. "Me? What about you?" I pointed at the guy standing beside him. "Did you know: That guy's a big crook."

The big crook said, "Tie him."

Bruno immediately grabbed me by the shoulder and shoved me so that I stumbled across the room and crashed into Liza.

"Sorry," I said. I turned, trying to regain my balance, but Bruno picked me up and slammed me down on the couch next to her.

"Hey!," I said. "Easy, darn it."

But he ignored my warning. Grabbing my hands he held them in front of me while the other goon, Simon, wrapped duck tape around my wrists.

I glared at Mr. Kimberly while he was doing it. "I'll bet you're in on this," I snarled. "You'll never get away with it."

239

Bruno and Simon moved away and the old guy, Parusko, came over and stopped in front of me. "You know who I am?" he said.

"Yeah." I tried to think how James Bond would handle this. "You're that big crook, Alfred Parusko."

Parusko put his face close to mine. "Who told you?"

Oh, oh. I should have played dumb. I certainly didn't want to tell him about Pepe. I squinted my eyes into a menacing glare. "Lucky guess," I said.

Parusko straightened. His menacing glare was a lot better than mine. "Which one is she?" he kind of whispered.

"Is who?" I answered.

"You been with 'em for more than a week. You gotta know."

Even if I knew which one was the golden girl, I wouldn't tell him. "I don't know what you're talking about," I lied.

Parusko turned to Bruno. "You ask him."

Bruno looked at me and grinned. I noticed he had really bad teeth. I suspected they got that way when he was a baby and cut his teeth on gun barrels.

Parusko stood back and Bruno moved in front of me. "I'm only going to ask you once."

I guess I kind of gulped, because Liza squirmed on the bench and tried to say something through the tape on her mouth. Bruno backhanded her across the cheek and a fiery rage shot through me. My hands had been fastened in front of me, and the way Bruno was bending forward his nose was a perfect target, and I smashed it with both fists.

With a grunt of pain, he reeled back. Catching his balance he straightened. He put his hands out, reaching for my throat. His glare was even better than Parusko's, and with blood seeping from his nose, he looked like the Frankenstein monster after being hit by that bolt of lightening.

Bruno grabbed me by the throat, and I was trying to think of which girl I should sacrifice when Bruno's interrogation was interrupted by a sailor charging into the cabin. He stopped in front of Parusko and without so much as a salute gasped out: "Sir. We're taking on water. We're going to have to abandon ship."

Parusko's face reddened so fast I thought he was having a heart attack or something. He looked at me and if I thought his glare had been a winner before, this one would have taken the gold metal. He shoved Bruno aside and his voice kind of exploded out like a blast of red-hot lava as he said, "What the shit have you done to my boat?"

My agile mind raced. "Me?" I said. I nodded toward Bruno and Simon. "It was them. Their car. Go look for yourself."

Parusko turned his glare on the two and they melted. "No, no," Simon yelped. "It was him. We had the SUV with the broads."

Parusko's glare swiveled back to me. "My boat sinks I'm gonna tear out your guts."

The sailor was right. The yacht was still moving but judging from the way I'd seen water coming in through the holes the car had created in the hull, the boat could very well be sinking. There was also another clue. I hesitated about calling attention to the fact that the floor had begun to tilt as the weight of water coming through the holes in the yacht's bow filled the front end. I had speared the yacht with the little yellow

241

car, but I didn't think it would sink it. Typically, I suppose I'd get blamed for that, too.

"It won't sink," I answered. "Untie my hands. I can fix it. I'm good with my hands. I can fix anything. Ask my mother. I once fixed a leak in our roof nobody else could even find." I looked at the sailor. "Have you got a can of 'Stop Leak'? Better make that two cans. Maybe a case."

The sailor said, "Huh?"

Bruno and Simon apparently noticed the floor's telltale tilt because they began edging toward the door. Simon glanced out one of portholes and his face paled. "We're in the ocean," he said. "We got lifeboats?"

I shot a glance out a porthole. He was right. The yacht was still moving along pretty fast which, actually, added to its death throes by forcing water into the shattered bow. Even so, we'd left the Barcelona port and were now in the Mediterranean Sea. Like Simon, I, too, wondered if yachts were equipped with lifeboats. Not that it mattered. I had a sneaking suspicion that the owner would like to see me go down with the ship, which didn't seem quite fair. After all, he was the captain.

Mr. Kimberly said, "We'd better get the girls up on deck."

Parusko kind of wiped his hand across his face in a gesture of futility. "Yeah, yeah." He jerked his head at the girls. "Get up on deck."

The girls were young and agile so it was no problem for them to get to their feet. Judging by the worried look in their eyes and their alacrity as they headed for the door, they believed the sailor was right when he'd said that old Ulysses was sinking.

I was directly behind Liza heading for the door

242

when Parusko grabbed my shoulder, jerking me back. "Not you," he said. His lack of compassion didn't surprise me, but it really got my goat when he also shoved Liza back. "You too," he said. "We don't need you."

Liza made a strangling sound behind the tape over her mouth and kicked at his crouch, but he'd already turned to the door so her kick landed on his thigh. He spun back and pushed her so hard she hit the wall and flopped on the couch.

I leaped to her side and was helping her to a sitting position when the cabin door slammed shut and I heard a lock snap.

I said, "Hold still," and yanked the tape off Liza's mouth.

"That bastard," she snarled. "I'm going to get his license."

"His name's Parusko," I said. "He's a criminal. They don't need licenses."

"Not him. Kimberly. He's been in on this from the beginning."

"Turn around," I said. When she stood up and turned around, I began working the duck tape off her wrists, at the same time saying, "I know. He's been trying to get me to find out which one it is."

Her hands were free now, and she started pulling the tape from my wrists.

"One what?" she said.

Oh, oh. Of course. She didn't know about the golden girl. Should I tell her? What good would that do now? It would just make her feel awful that Mr. Kimberly had asked me to learn the identity of the golden girl instead of her. So I said, "I think he told that guy Parusko the girls all came from rich American

243

families. They hatched a scheme to kidnap all of them. We kind of got caught in the middle."

She had my hands free now, and to my surprise she put her hands behind my head and kissed me.

"Wow," I said. "What was that for?"

"Trying to rescue us."

I was kind of hoping for another reward, but she moved to the door. "We're not too far from the harbor," she said. "Are you a good swimmer?"

"I am when it counts." I got to the door ahead of her and tried to open it. As I expected, it was locked. "If we can't get out of here, I'll never find out."

By this time the deck had a decided tilt and she said, "We'll have to break it down."

She tried to pick up one of the chairs near the table but it was anchored to the floor. I moved to help her when I heard a 'whoop, whoop, whoop' sound.

"Police boat," I chortled. "They'll get us."

"They'd better hurry," she said.

"Good point." If the police didn't know we were locked in the cabin, they might not force the door. I yanked at the chair and Liza joined me. I guess it was the strength of desperation, but we managed to wrench it free. Using it as a battering ram we broke through the door and scrambled out on deck.

The yacht's engine had stopped and it was dead in the water with it's bow almost under water. A big police boat was stopped a few feet away and they were pulling Bruno and Simon out of the water. A small police boat was closing in on a lifeboat from the yacht that was holding a couple of sailors, Mr. Kimberly, Parusko and the girls, who were still tied. I almost expected to see Parusko throw them overboard in an attempt to get rid of the evidence. But with the police closing in, it was a little late for that.

And the big police boat was now heading for the sinking yacht where Liza and I had climbed to the roof of the cabin. Pepe stood in the bow of the police boat like a figurehead from heaven. When he saw us, he waved. Putting his hands to his mouth to form a megaphone he called, "Need some help?"

I put an arm around Liza's waist. "Not us," I called. "We were just about to take them all."

Pepe laughed. I sure was glad to see him.

CHAPTER 25

A few hectic days later on a balmy evening in Madrid's Plaza Major musicians were blaring out music for a Folkloric Festival. The music blasted off the surrounding buildings and dancers cavorted all over the place while waiters, with their distinctive white aprons tied around their waists, somehow wove their way through boisterous crowds while precariously balancing trays above their heads with one hand, trays loaded with liquids, *tapas* and succulent dishes of food.

Adding to the festivities, a constant influx of magicians, dancers, and costumed performers carved out niches in the crowds for performances that nobody seemed to be watching.

I don't know how she did it but Liza had managed to secure a table in the heart of the Plaza for the two of us and Pepe. The girls would have been with us, but after their rescue in Barcelona and after we had all endured hours of interrogation by the *policia*, their anxious parents had insisted they all return to their homes in America.

The girls hadn't put up too many objections, especially when I explained to them how during our last few days we were scheduled to explore historic castles and cathedrals in such exotic places as Zaragosa and Santiago de Compostela. I had even thrown in an entire afternoon at the Universidad in Salamanca. But, somehow, their lives in such exotic places as Tucson, Oklahoma City, Los Angeles and St. Louis didn't sem so mundane to them anymore, and they had elected to return home.

Now, sitting in Madrid's pulsating Plaza Major

with Liza and Pepe, assaulted by competing musical bands, drinking sparkling grape juice and eating tapas, proved to be astonishingly relaxing, at least to me.

"The whole thing,"—Pepe had almost to shout to be heard—"was a big mistake."

"A mistake?" Liza said.

Pepe nodded. "Apparently Kimberly got the idea when those four ladies booked the tour with him that one of them was the daughter of some billionaire. He contacted Parusko and they worked out a plan to kidnap the girl as soon as they found out which one it was."

"I knew something was wrong from the beginning," Liza said. "Even talking to Mr. Kimberly before we started, something didn't seem right."

"It was all a big mistake," Pepe said. "There was no billionaire's daughter."

I chimed in with a bit of astute analysis: "Those two guys we thought were paparazzi worked for Parusko,"

Pepe said, "Right. They were supposed to grab the girl as soon as they found out which one she was."

"The thing I don't understand," Liza said, "is how they knew where we were all the time."

"Well,---"Pepe began to say.

I interrupted, explaining, "Mr. Kimberly had a copy of our itinerary."

"Only the cities," Liza said. "I don't know how he knew the exact places we covered."

I guess I had a guilty look because Liza stared at me as she said, "Did you report to Mr. Kimberly."

There it was again: my fault. I tap danced around the implication: "He wanted me to call him...every day, but...." I smiled as though I had been too smart to fall for Mr. Kimberly's diabolic plan. "I didn't do it. Not every day."

"It really didn't matter," Pepe said. "He had a backup."

I tried to hide my dumbfound heart. "A backup?"

Pepe nodded. "I figured it had to be you or her."

"I'm innocent," I said. "It was her."

"Her?" Liza said.

"Who?" I said.

"Maria," Pepe said. "Kimberly told her to keep in touch with him."

"Kimberly told her." I was shocked, shocked, to think that Mr. Kimberly didn't trust me. "I was supposed to do that."

"Maria!" Liza said. "She was working with that man, Parusko? I don't believe it."

"She didn't know about him. Kimberly told her those two goons were secret bodyguards for the girls. She didn't know what was going on."

Liza gave a small sigh of relief. "So it wasn't her fault."

"Correct. She thought she was doing the right thing."

"But you...," I said astutely. "Why would Kimberly Tours hire you. You're a policeman."

Pepe laughed. "We've been watching Parusko. We found out he was up to something regarding your tour. We persuaded the real Pepe to let me take his place."

"So," I quickly deduced. "Pepe isn't your real name?"

"No. Inspector Raul Carona, Madrid *policia*." He got up and handed Liza and me business cards.

"Next time you're in Madrid, give me a call."

"Okay," I said. I scribbled my name and phone number on the back of his card as I said, "And next time you're in Phoenix...," ---I handed him the card---- "give me a call."

He took the card and tucked it in his shirt pocket. "Will do. And for now..." He lifted Liza's hand and, with a little bow, kissed it. "*Hasta la vista*," he said. "Enjoy Spain."

Liza and I watched him weave through the crowd until we lost him like the end of a dream.

Liza and I sat in silence for a moment. I didn't know about her, but I felt a wondrous release from tons of anxiety that I didn't realize I'd been carrying since we'd begun our tour. There was just one little nagging worry.

"With Mr. Kimberly in jail," I said, "how are we going to get paid?"

She thought about that for a moment, stirring her sparkling mineral water with a swizzle stick. "The tour was all paid for in advance, including our transportation, so we won't have any problems with money." Without looking up, she said, "As for our jobs and our salaries.... I guess there won't be a Kimberly Tours anymore. We'll have to look for other jobs."

"At another tour company?"

"I guess so. I enjoy the work: seeing the world, meeting people. That's why I took the job in the first place. What about you?"

"Well, the summer is still young. I'll need another summer job. But another tour? I doubt I could take another one."

She kind of laughed before she reached across the table and turned my hand over, her fingers lightly

249

caressing my palm. "How about continuing this one....with me?"

I sat, frozen with amazement. Under the caress of her hand, my own hand had to be burning a hole through the table top. My mouth tried to make sounds of joy, but all it could muster was a stupid, "With...with you?"

She leaned forward, her exquisite lips forming an exquisite smile. Her exquisite eyes stole my gaze with burning intensity; her exquisite hair, framing her exquisite face, spilled to her exquisite shoulders, highlighting the exquisite smile that would not release my stunned mind.

"Romantic Spain," she whispered. "Just the two of us. Would you come with me?"

Would I? Alone? Romantic Spain? With Liza? If I hadn't been so stunned, I would have yelped for joy. I would go with her to Hades. My shell-shocked brain could hardly get words into my mouth quick enough. "Yes. Yes, yes."

"Wonderful," she whispered. "We'll see all the sights, dance all the dances, walk on the beach under Mediterranean stars, have a wonderful time."

Exotic images caused my eyes to lose focus, but my intellectual brain betrayed me. It made my voice stammer, "I can't. I don't have any money."

Her hand curled around mine. "Don't worry about that," she said, and her exquisite lips curled into a wicked smile. "After all, my father is one of the richest men in the world."

HER father. It was HER! OMG.

The End.

Made in the USA
San Bernardino, CA
18 November 2015